WEB OF LIES

Dr. C. White-Elliott

This book is a work of fiction. It was created from the author's imagination. Any similarity to actual events is purely coincidental.

CLF Publishing, LLC.
9161 Sierra Ave, Ste. 203C
Fontana, CA 92335
www.clfpublishing.org

Cover design by *Senir Design*. Contact information- info@senirdesign.com.

ISBN # 978-1-945102-20-2

Printed in the United States of America.

Dedication

This book is dedicated to my son Daron White, who is my co-conspirator. His vivid imagination helped me to sort out my ideas and allowed this book to come to fruition.

We had a great time spinning this tale, and to him, I am thankful.

1

On Thursday, January 23, Judge Marilyn Hanson's courtroom, of the San Francisco Superior Court, was filled to capacity with television crews from all the major news stations and curious members of the local community. They wanted to get first-hand information about who was responsible for the death of Charlito Jimenez, a prominent business owner who had been murdered in his home. He was well respected in the community, for he had been resourceful in raising funds for scholarships for under-privileged youth to play sports and achieve their academic collegiate desires.

Although his death was nearly a year ago, the police had finally gathered enough evidence against his wife Brenda Jimenez to bring a case against her, causing her to stand trial before a jury of her peers. Court had been in session for three days so far. To date, police detectives and a forensic analyst had provided evidence for the prosecution.

In the audience, the onlookers consisted of those who sided with the district attorney's office, as well as those who believed in the innocence of the defendant. Charlito and Brenda Jimenez had been married for over twenty years and had never shown signs of discord to anyone. So, those who knew them could not imagine Brenda causing harm to her husband - let alone killing him.

As Tinisha Salisbury, attorney at law for the defense, stood near the witness stand, she interrogated the prosecutor's witness about what he saw on the night of the fatal shooting. Outwardly, the witness looked confident, yet on the inside he wondered what he had gotten himself into by testifying. When the police had questioned the Jimenez's neighbors, he had only shared with them what he had recalled seeing, not thinking it would lead to him being on the witness stand.

Looking directly at Tinisha, and avoiding Brenda's hard stare, he answered each question truthfully. But each time Tinisha asked him a question and he answered, she always had a follow-up question, but he remained poised. He looked very dapper in his mint green dress shirt, brown slacks, and brown loafers. His dark hair was neatly parted on one side and not a hair was out of place. His smile was pleasant and his demeanor respectable.

During the lively exchange of questions and answers between Tinisha and the prosecutor's witness, Tinisha's husband Rafael Salisbury walked through the courtroom doors and stood quietly watching his wife. Rafael loved to see Tinisha tear into witnesses, like a lioness on the prowl. But, it was rare that he had the pleasure to do so due to the responsibilities of his position in law enforcement. He admired her professional growth.

Over the years, just as he had become more proficient in enforcing law codes and the law's various other aspects, he had witnessed his wife's confidence grow, as she perfected her interrogation techniques. He marveled at her ability to draw answers from a witness or anyone for that matter, even him.

Studying Rafael's demeanor, Judge Hanson knew it was rare for Captain Salisbury to be in the courtroom because of his job responsibilities, so she concluded his presence was urgent. As Tinisha continued to question the witness, Judge Hanson beckoned for Rafael to approach the short gate that led to the lawyers' tables.

As Rafael stood wearing his perfectly pressed uniform with his captain's shield and stripes, his posture was completely erect and his hands were clasped behind his back. As his presence served as an interruption, try as they might, some spectators could not remove their eyes from Rafael's back to focus on the witness who was sitting on the witness stand. Rafael's very presence, nonofficial as it was in the courtroom, demanded attention.

In her peripheral vision, Tinisha saw the judge gesture, but she knew it was not directed towards her, so she did not break her concentration as she focused on backing the witness into a corner with her last set of questions. She knew she had to create a sense of doubt in the jurors' minds about the accuracy and/or truthfulness of the testimony the witness had provided.

"Did you actually see the defendant, Mrs. Jimenez, in the driver seat of the car you saw pulling from the driveway early Monday morning?"

"No, ma'am. I did not," the witness responded, as though he were perturbed with her line of questioning.

"Did you see Brenda Jimenez anywhere in the vehicle?"

"No, ma'am. I did not."

"Who was driving the vehicle?"

"I don't know. I could not see the driver from where I was seated inside the taxi."

"So, when you gave your statement to the police, you assumed she was driving because you saw a car that was the same make and model as Mrs. Jimenez's car?" Tinisha asked almost accusingly.

"Well, I didn't assume it was her car. I *know* it was her car because it had her license plate," the witness said matter-of-factly, slightly raising his voice.

"You committed her license plate to memory?" Tinisha queried, finding his behavior out of the ordinary.

"Sure. It says Go Getter- G-O-G-E-T-T-R," he spelled.

A hush fell over the crowd. No one moved, and no one said a word. But their eyes moved curiously between the defendant and the witness, as they wondered about the truth of the matter. Everyone wanted to know if Brenda was driving the car or not.

As Brenda listened to the witness' testimony, her back stiffened. She felt so alone. She had no one. No husband. No children. No siblings. No one to offer her support. The few friends she did have had been distant and offered no explanation whatsoever. She took their absence to mean they thought she was guilty or at least knew more than she was letting on. She did not understand how they could take that position. But, one thing was obvious- they did not want to be associated with her- in public or private. Their actions had made that abundantly clear. In her mind, all of her friends had known her for years, and from her perspective, they should have known she would never physically harm a soul. The one friend she could always count on was no longer there, and that hurt her heart more than anything.

Without looking at her client, Tinisha kept her gaze fixed on the witness as she made her final statement. "But, I repeat- you did not see the defendant Brenda Jimenez in the vehicle." The witness knew Tinisha's words did not come in the form of a question, so he remained quiet.

Having finished questioning the witness, Tinisha followed her statement with a look at the judge and by saying, "I have no further questions for this witness," as she tugged lightly at the bottom of her navy blue suit jacket, allowing her hands to slowly slide down the sides of her skirt, as if she were pressing invisible wrinkles from it.

As Tinisha began to walk back to her table being careful not to look questioningly at her client, she noticed her husband standing at the gate. She glanced over to the judge to ask to be excused, but before her request could be made, Judge Hanson simply waved her hand in Tinisha's direction, letting her know to go ahead and find out what had prompted her husband's presence.

As soon as Tinisha's and Rafael's eyes met, Tinisha knew her husband's presence was of a serious nature. Otherwise, he certainly would not have interrupted her work-in court or out. However, she couldn't gather her thoughts quickly enough to presuppose what could possibly have happened to cause him to appear at the courthouse that day without prior warning. But, she had an eerie feeling the news would not be pleasant.

As soon as she was near him, Rafael held his wife close as he stood on one side of the gate and she stood on the other. He whispered softly into her ear, "Your father has been rushed to the emergency room at S. F. Memorial. He had a heart attack."

When she heard the news, her body immediately lost its erect posture, as her knees went weak, and she fell into her husband's chest. A sound escaped from her mouth, and her hand immediately went up to try to control her gasp. The members of the audience let out gasps and sighs, as they wondered what Rafael had said to Tinisha. They wondered if it was related to the case or if it was personal.

Tinisha's eyes met Rafael's again, as she searched for answers, without verbalizing her questions. Looking at her intently, Rafael replied softly to her unasked question, "He's in surgery." Quickly, Tinisha regained her composure and turned to the judge and said, "I need an immediate recess for the rest of the afternoon. My father is in the hospital. It's an emergency, Your Honor."

As tears began to fill Tinisha's eyes, Judge Hanson immediately raised her gavel and said, "Court will stand in recess until tomorrow morning at 10am." To Tinisha, she responded, "By all means. And know that I wish Pastor Oglebee well."

Tinisha's father was a well-known pastor in the local community. He had served in several capacities of ministry over the past forty plus years, from chaplain of various organizations, to pastor of the church he founded, to family confidante. People knew him by name. Tinisha had a reputation of her own- in and out of the courtroom. The community also knew Tinisha had served as the youth pastor while she was in law school. Occasionally, she still preached when her father called on her, which was approximately every two to three months, unless a case had her tied up.

Tinisha gave a slight nod to Judge Hanson to thank her for her kindness and understanding. She could not speak loudly due to the lump that was developing in her throat. She quickly gathered her belongings from the table, stuffed them into her briefcase, and told her client she would call her later that evening.

The bailiff yelled out, "All rise!" Everyone stood as the judge rose from her seat and exited the courtroom. The bailiff, sensing the urgency of Tinisha's situation, prevented those who came to watch the trial from leaving the courtroom until Tinisha and Rafael had exited. Together, the power couple nearly ran from the courtroom to Rafael's car, and he drove as quickly as he could, without breaking speed laws, to get his wife to the hospital to see her father.

Once the crowd had exited the court-room, the last two people to leave were the defendant Brenda Jimenez, Tinisha's client, and Javier Robles, the witness for the state who had just stepped down from the witness stand. When Javier tried to approach Brenda, she picked up her pace. She had nothing to say to him because she felt he had deliberately lied when he said he saw her car pulling out of her driveway during the same time frame the coroner had given for the approximate time of her husband's death. Javier eventually caught up with Brenda by the time she had reached her car. She was surprised because she thought she had lost him in the crowd. *I couldn't be so lucky*, she thought.

When she pushed the button on the remote to unlock the doors of her cherry-red Mercedes CLA coupe, she opened the driver side door and got in. Javier, desperate to speak with her, quickly went to the passenger side and got into the front seat next to her, not waiting to ask permission. Painfully, he knew he would be rejected, so he took matters into his own hands. Brenda wanted to yell for help, but at the same time, she wanted to know why Javier had lied. Plus, she really did not believe he planned to cause her any harm. She had her own ideas about why he had lied to the police, but she wanted to hear his reasons from him.

"Javier, what is going on?" Brenda asked, not giving him an opportunity to speak.

"I don't understand why you are upset. What did I do wrong?" Javier questioned with a dumbfounded look on his face, obviously not realizing how damning his testimony was.

"I don't understand why you lied on the stand, saying you saw me leaving my house when I wasn't even there."

Javier lifted a finger to interrupt and quiet Brenda. "First of all, I didn't say I saw you. Secondly, I said I saw your car pulling out of the driveway. And, I know what I saw."

"Saying you saw my car is the same as saying you saw me! Who else would be driving my car? As long as you have known me and Charlie, you know we hardly ever switched cars."

"Look… all I know is I saw your car."

Basically ignoring his last statement, Brenda said, "Javier, after all we have been through, I don't understand how you could do this to me. Are you upset because I broke it off and told you I wanted to work it out with Charlie?"

"Brenda, of course not. Wait… Yes, I was upset, but I certainly wouldn't lie to the police about what I saw, and I definitely wouldn't try to cause any harm to you. So, if you weren't there, where were you?"

"Well, frankly that's none of your business!"

"You know- that's one thing I never liked about you. You have too many secrets!"

"Well, I guess you don't have to worry about that now do you?" she asked snappishly, with a roll of her eyes.

"Well, I guess you are right about that, but right now this is not personal. This is not about us. This is about keeping you out of jail!" Javier responded, in an elevated voice.

"Keeping me out of jail?" Brenda shouted. "Your testimony just might help to send me TO jail!"

"Brenda, I know you are upset, but being angry with me isn't helping," Javier said patiently, while lowering his voice and allowing Brenda to vent. "I don't understand why you can't share your whereabouts with me. You know I still love you, Bren," he said, cutting her name short, using the pet name he had for her. "I would never break your confidence," he added with a smile.

"Yes, I know you are right, and it's not a big secret. I was with Virginia at her treatment. And afterward, I went to her home for the rest of the weekend."

"Well, did you let someone borrow your car? Because I know I saw your car backing out of the driveway at about three-thirty in the morning because I was just getting in from the bar," he said, continuing to press the issue. Ever since Javier's wife had been battling cancer, Javier had begun frequenting the bar to get a little stress relief. He knew drinking wasn't the answer, but it worked for him during that stressful and sorrowful time.

"No, I did not let anyone borrow my car. As a matter fact, I didn't even have my car. My car was in the shop."

"Well, why didn't your lawyer bring that up in court to discredit my testimony?"

"I didn't get a chance to tell her. I had no idea you were going to say you saw my car or me. You know, this whole thing is very confusing and very frustrating. I cannot believe I am being accused of murdering my own husband. We may not have been getting along very well, but I certainly did not want him dead!"

After Brenda and Javier's brief talk, Javier quietly exited her vehicle, wondering if Brenda would ever open up to him again. Absentmindedly, he walked to his black Ford F150, as he allowed fond memories of the times they shared together to fill his mind.

Smiling to himself, even with feelings of regret, he exited the parking garage and drove home to his family. He knew his wife would have many questions about court-even from her sick bed. He knew she was aware of the affinity he had for Brenda, even if she hadn't said so. He knew his wife would want him to live happily after she was gone although she would not have wanted him to break up anyone's marriage to gain that happiness.

Meanwhile, Brenda took a moment to dry her eyes and collect herself. She was in no particular hurry. She did not have anyone at home waiting for her. Quite frankly, she did not feel at home in her own house. Someone had violated her space.

Over the past year, she contemplated finding somewhere else to live. At the same time, she couldn't find it in herself to leave. She and Charlie had made so many memories there, and the bottom line was- it was her home.

Without waiting for Rafael's white Range Rover to come to a complete stop at the emergency room entrance, Tinisha unbuckled the seat belt, grabbed her purse, flung the car door open, and bolted through the emergency room doors. Rafael knew it would be a waste of time to chastise her about being careful. He understood how she must be feeling. He recalled having had the same feeling when he was unexpectedly called to the hospital for both his parents, at their respective time of passing.

On the short drive over there, Tinisha had rested her head against the cushioned headrest, as she tried to avoid the sun as it glared through the window and beamed against her face. She had scarcely needed the pack of tissue her husband had given her because the sun had dried her tears as soon as they had fallen, which was odd for that time of year when the rain is usually pouring down. Other than the sound of a few sniffles, she had been virtually quiet, except for when she placed a brief call to Delores, her mother. Once her mother had answered the phone, Tinisha didn't have to ask what had happened to her father or inquire about his present prognosis. Diligently, her mother had begun to fill her in as soon as the call was connected.

Earlier that day, during the late morning, her mother and father had been sitting in the family room of their home, playing a hand of their favorite game, Scrabble, trying to outwit one another with their word choices. They had not too long finished a late break-fast that had consisted of homemade biscuits smothered with sausage gravy, sunny side up eggs, thick slices of bacon, and cups of hot coffee complete with dairy creamer. Delores only allowed her husband such indulgences ever so often. But not often enough as far as he was concerned.

About halfway through the game, Richard groaned, grabbed his chest, and fell over, without saying a word. To her touch, his skin was clammy, and his breathing was labored. Delores knew the signs all too well. She immediately jumped up, ran to the phone, and dialed 911. Emergency personnel only took seven minutes to arrive and carted him directly to the hospital. Delores elected not to ride in the ambulance. Instead, she followed close behind in her car, not knowing how long she would be there and if she would need to go back home for any reason.

Once inside the emergency room doors, Tinisha spotted the nurses' station and quickly made her way over to the short blonde who was wearing a colorful nurse's uniform. Just as she was about to inquire about her father's condition, she heard her mother's voice calling her name. Tinisha quickly turned around, facing her mother. They immediately embraced one another. Tinisha felt hot tears streaming down from her eyes.

"Mom," she said, "Dad..." And that was all she could utter. Her mother understood her broken sentences and began to reassure her by saying, "Don't worry. Your father is going to be okay. He's a fighter. He's in surgery right now. The doctors are performing a triple bypass," as she wiped away the tears from her daughter's eyes.

"Oh, Mom. This is so serious. Do you think the surgery will solve the problem? I don't want him to go through this again; you know this is not his first heart attack." Tinisha sounded nearly hysterical. All professionalism had left as soon as she left the courtroom. It was as though she had become a little girl all over again. She could not imagine anything happening to either one of her parents. She couldn't bear the thought.

"Think positive thoughts. He is in the Lord's hands. All we can do now is pray, baby." The few nurses who were positioned at the station watched the exchange between mother and daughter, and their hearts went out to them, just as they did for all the patients that came through the emergency room doors.

As the nurses sat observing, one of them looked up at the television that was mounted on the wall and back to Tinisha. Then, her head turned to the screen again. She tapped her colleague on the arm and pointed towards the television. He understood what she was trying to convey, and he simply nodded his head. The court case was being televised, and there was Tinisha- live and in living color. As Delores was consoling her daughter, she picked up on the topic of the non-verbal conversation that was flowing between the nurses.

Slowly, Delores guided Tinisha to the family waiting room where she had been planted since her husband had been brought by ambulance to the emergency room and subsequently taken into surgery.

The waiting room was cozy and was decorated with couches and reclining chairs, instead of individual seats. The hospital's administration realized patients' families sometimes spent long hours waiting to hear the condition of their loved ones and even came in during all hours of the day and night. Waiting could be exhausting, so the administration wanted their extended guests to be as comfortable as possible.

As they sat, Delores continued to console her daughter, and Tinisha tried to return the favor, thinking about how her mother must be feeling when her husband of over thirty-eight years was undergoing a surgical procedure he could very well not live through.

Not long after, Rafael appeared in the doorway of the waiting room. When he spotted his wife and mother-in-law, he quickly took a seat next to his wife and covered one of her hands with his own, in an earnest attempt to comfort her, fully aware that his attempt may go unfruitful. Tinisha leaned her head onto his shoulder and closed her eyes. She truly did not know what to make of the situation. That was the second time her father had had a heart attack.

The first time was approximately five years prior, but he didn't suffer much at all, and surgery had not been required. However, she and her mother knew he needed a life-style change as it related to his eating patterns and the level of stress he carried on a day-to-day basis as a pastor. Since then, he had not changed much in the way of his pastoralship; however, he had made great headway in changing his eating patterns with the help and constant insistence of his wife. He was on a low-carb diet, had his full servings of fruits and vegetables daily, and only ate red meat once or twice a month, which included ground beef, which he had tried to convince his wife was 'brown' meat.

Breaking the silence, Rafael asked, "How long has Dad been in surgery?" Tinisha looked to her mother for the answer.

"Forty-eight minutes," Delores answered matter-of-factly, after glancing at her watch.

Rafael smiled at Delores' precise answer. Daily, he heard the same precision of time from his wife. That was one of the many similarities the two women shared.

"Did the doctor say how long the surgery will actually take?"

"Approximately two to three hours," she answered.

"Okay, ladies," Rafael started. Both women looked at him intently. "I am going to make a proposition, and I want you both to take me seriously," he said, trying to proceed gingerly.

"What is it?" Tinisha asked softly.

"Well, we have another hour or two for Dad to be in surgery, and I think it's best if we go downstairs to the cafeteria and get a bite to eat. We can come right back up afterward to get an update on his prognosis."

"I really don't..." Tinisha started to say, but her mother interjected.

"Rafael is right. We could just sit here and do nothing, but we all need to take care of our health and strength, so I think that's a good idea, Son. Plus, I'm sure you haven't eaten all day because you were in court. You know you must take good care of yourself, Tinisha. So, let's go."

Reluctantly, Tinisha rose to her feet, fully comprehending it was two against one. She took one of her mother's hands into her own and her husband's hand into her other hand, as they proceeded to the elevator. She was overwhelmed with the enormity of the weight of the trial on her shoulders, and now, her father's condition only added to her stress. In the elevator, Rafael took the middle position and held both women closely, comforting them with his broad shoulders. Quietly, they rode the elevator down to the basement, where the hospital cafeteria was located.

When Rafael, Tinisha, and Delores had made it to the cafeteria, they walked over to the serving line to get a hot meal. Tinisha opted for mushroom gravy covered meatloaf, a side of garlic mashed potatoes, and mixed vegetables. Her mother also chose the meatloaf but with a side of rice pilaf and string beans. Rafael chose baked tilapia, rice pilaf, and corn.

Tinisha glanced quickly at her husband's plate, noting it was void of anything green. She shot him a disapproving look, and he pretended not to see her watching him. She knew he did not care much for green vegetables, but he consumed them when she pressed the issue. He knew under the present circumstances he could skate by, as her focus was primarily elsewhere.

Ten minutes into the meal, Rafael's cell phone rang, with a call coming in from the police station. "Captain Salisbury," Rafael answered.

"Hey, Cap. Sorry to bother you. I know you're at the hospital with your wife, but we just got a call from the fire department about a fire, possibly arson, over on Billings Road. The chief of police is requesting your presence at the scene."

"What's the urgency, and why did the FD call us?" Rafael inquired, as he continued enjoying his meal.

"They found a body. They haven't been able to identify the victim yet, but so far one employee and the owner have not been accounted for. The coroner took the body to the morgue. He will begin processing the victim's dental work to see if he can possibly make an identification."

"Where exactly was the fire?"

"At Firestone."

"The tire shop?"

"Exactly."

"I will be there in thirty minutes. Have Detectives Milford and Gonzalez meet me there."

"Will do, Cap."

Before Rafael could explain to his wife and mother-in-law what the call was about, Tinisha piped up and began her inquiry.

"What was that about?"

"There was a fire at a tire shop and a body was found. I need to head over there now. I will be back just as soon as I can."

"Is the fire still going, or did the fire department put it out already?" Delores asked.

"I'm not sure," Rafael answered.

"Honey, be careful," Tinisha pleaded, thinking about the potential danger he could face, a danger for which he was not professionally trained.

"I will," Rafael reassured her, as he stood up from the table. He grabbed his plate, preparing to take it over to the trash dispenser, but Delores put her hand on the side of it and said, "We will take care of it. Go ahead, Son." Kissing his wife with a quick peck on the lips, and one to Delores' cheek, Rafael departed.

As Rafael walked to the elevator, Tinisha saw a familiar gleam in her mother's eyes, as Delores watched Rafael. Her mother had always admired and respected Rafael and was honored to have him as a son-in-law, but to her, he had always been more than that.

Even before Tinisha and Rafael were married, Delores had always called Rafael-Son. Tinisha was her parents' only child, and they both had welcomed Rafael with open arms. Because his parents were already deceased, his wife's family gave him the family he had been missing for quite a while.

After Tinisha and Delores finished their meal, they returned to the family waiting room and found another family there: a father with three young children, one of whom was curled up in one of the recliners fast asleep.

After Delores inquired about their situation, having introduced herself to the father and telling him about her husband's heart attack and subsequent surgery, he told them that his wife was pregnant with twins and had gone into labor, but once they arrived to the hospital, the doctor had found that one of the baby's umbilical cord was wrapped around its neck.

That baby was positioned closer to the cervix than its twin, so the lives of both babies were being threatened, as the first one could not be delivered without risk of strangulation. The doctor was performing an emergency C-section, and the father and the three children were just waiting to hear the news.

While Delores continued the discourse with Albert, the father, she eventually began to pray for him, his wife, and their unborn children. Tears began to fill his eyes as well as the eyes of two of the three children who sat quietly nearby, listening to the prayers go up for their mother and their unborn siblings. They were very grateful that someone would take the focus off her own situation and place so much attention on theirs. Tinisha sat quietly watching her mother in action, as Delores took advantage of an opportunity to show compassion to someone else in a time when her own heart must have been heavy.

As she listened to her mother pour out love on the family, her cell phone rang, but the caller ID only stated "Unknown." Her first inclination was to ignore the call and allow it to go to voicemail. She really did not feel like talking. But, her intuition told her to answer the call. After all, it was still during business hours. Also, with the ringing of the phone, she realized she had not called her boss to give him an update on court that day or her emergency departure. She definitely wanted to call and apprise him of the details before he saw it on the evening news, as the case was being covered.

"Salisbury," Tinisha answered softly.

On the other end of the call, a voice asked, "Tinisha Salisbury?"

"Yes," Tinisha responded.

"This is Caroline, Judge Hanson's executive assistant. She asked me to give you a call to let you know court will be postponed until Monday morning at 10 AM. She realizes you are dealing with a delicate situation, and she wants to give you time over the weekend to prepare yourself and your client for court on Monday as you deal with your father's health issues."

Tinisha nearly burst into tears, but she held them back. "Please tell Judge Hanson thank you for me. I will be in court promptly on Monday morning."

After disconnecting the call, Tinisha immediately called her boss and spoke with him briefly. He offered a compassionate response. Then, she dialed Brenda Jimenez. The call went to voicemail. Tinisha told her about the postponement and simply stated, "I will call you sometime tomorrow, and I need you to explain the whereabouts of your car on the day your husband was murdered." She ended the message by explaining why she had to leave court abruptly.

****

When Captain Salisbury made it to the scene of the fire, Detectives Milford and Gonzalez were already there taking samples from the scene along with the fire department personnel, who were beginning to suspect arson. Deciding not to interrupt their work and spotting the fire captain, Rafael made his way over through the maze of people. Captain Lynn Fitzgerald spotted Rafael, as they had met on a few occasions before, and waved him over.

As Rafael walked towards the fire captain, he took in the entire scene. One third of the roof was gone. The metal bay doors were singed, but the cars inside were burned from the inside out. The customer waiting room and the office where the body had been found were badly burned. The smell was strong, and Rafael knew it could be smelled from miles around. It would be days before the ashes stopped lingering in the air.

Reaching Lynn, Rafael extended his hand as a manner of greeting. "Captain Salisbury," she said with a large grin across her face as if though she was greeting a long-time friend she had not seen for some time.

"So, nice to see you. Sorry the circumstances aren't better," she said shaking his hand firmly.

"Same here, Captain Fitzgerald," Rafael responded cordially, as he released his hand from hers, noticing a slight reluctance on her part. "So, what have you learned so far?"

"Well, as you know a body was found. It is unidentifiable at present. We attempted to narrow down the possibilities by getting a list of employees. We were able to get the list along with employees' telephone numbers from the owner's daughter. She is the payroll clerk."

"So, you still haven't been able to locate the owner?"

"That's correct. His name is Joshua Middleton. And the other employee that is unaccounted for is Ryan Stone. But, we left messages on both their voicemails and one with the owner's wife, Melanie. As far as we know, from Joshua's daughter, Ryan is not married, and he does not have a home phone."

"Yeah, most people don't nowadays," Rafael said almost to himself. "And who is to say the body belongs to someone who works here. Couldn't it have also been the person who set the fire, if it is indeed arson?"

"Yes, of course. That is absolutely true, but not likely."

Rafael raised his eyebrows at Lynn's response, but he did not interrupt.

"We did discover a scrap of the shirt that had not burned, and the name patch is visible, except the name is not legible. It matches the shirts found in the employee lockers. So, we are pretty sure the body is that of an employee or the owner."

"I see," Rafael murmured. "Okay, next question."

"Shoot," Lynn said, eager to engage in the meeting of the minds.

"What makes you think it was arson?"

"Well, first we checked the outlets to see if there was faulty wiring, or if an appliance or other machinery, in the case of a business such as this, pulled an electrical charge too strong for the outlet causing sparks to fly or malfunction. There was no evidence of either."

"Okay," Rafael nodded as he listened intently, as he kicked around pieces of rubble with the toe of his department standard issue shoes.

"From there, we inspected the perimeter of the building and found traces of gasoline."

"It isn't odd for a tire shop to house gasoline, though," Rafael interjected.

"True, true. But it is odd for gasoline to be found in the cracks of concrete around the perimeter. The arsonist may have thought the fire would cover up all traces of the gasoline, but concrete does not burn, and the gas that fell in the cracks was easily detected."

"Well, I will have my guys dust door-knobs and the gas can for fingerprints."

"I believe they are already on it. I saw your fingerprint technician pull up a few minutes before you arrived."

"Great eye," Rafael complimented.

"Of course," Lynn said, as she eyed Rafael from head to toe. Rafael picked up on her subtle move but decided against addressing her. Although Rafael had only met Lynn on a few occasions, he had heard about her around town and also from his wife, who was once a classmate of Lynn's. Lynn was divorced and would frequently be seen around town with different men. Most of her attempts at dating were unfruitful because, unfortunately, some men had a problem dealing with a woman who commanded respect with her very presence and stood in a position of authority in a profession that was dominated by men.

She had definitely broken barriers, and she was no pushover. She stood strong and did not waver in her decisions. She knew what she wanted and what needed to be done in a given situation. That is what had caused her fast promotion to the position of captain, after serving as a firefighter for only seven years. However, there were some who speculated about her promotion, but they had no evidence to support anything to the contrary.

After Rafael excused himself from Lynn's presence, he conferred with the police detectives and the fingerprint tech. Shortly after, he made his departure. He was anxious to return to the hospital to be by his wife's side. He wanted to be there if she should need him. He was confident he would receive updates about the fire and the victim as the case progressed, so he did not feel the need to be present for first-hand updates.

As Rafael started his car and pulled out of the parking lot, he did another visual survey of the building and the damage the fire had managed to do. All he could do was shake his head and wonder what the person's motive was for setting the fire and if it was intended for homicide to take place as well, or if the person was simply a casualty of the fire- a case of being in the wrong place at the wrong time.

Driving down the street, Rafael's mind shifted from the fire back to the hospital where he had left his wife. He knew she was consumed with worry and concern for her father. He was concerned as well. Pastor Richard Oglebee was no spring chicken and his heart condition was obviously not good. But, as Rafael's mother-in-law had said, "He's in the Lord's hands." So, they would just have to keep the faith.

3

On Friday morning at 6:30, in Portola, a subset of San Francisco, Bernie Matheson and his wife of fourteen years, Josephine, along with their two teenage children, Cathy, who was sixteen years old, and her younger brother Ivan, who was thirteen years old, sat at the breakfast table quietly. The atmosphere in the Matheson's home was usually easygoing and fun loving. Neither the parents nor the children were ever stiff or pretentious. All were comfortable in their own skin, and it reflected in their personalities.

Their home furnishings as well as their clothing showed their lower middle-class lifestyle. The furniture was worn and even had a few tears, but none of the Mathesones minded so much. They were far more interested in genuine happiness and family unity, which they had built with a steady flow of communication, even after the children experienced the extended absence of their father some years ago.

While most teenagers were usually at each other's throats, Cathy and Ivan had a tight-knit relationship. When they weren't with their respective friends, they spent time together sharing the events of their day. And if something were troubling one of them, they would knock on the other's bedroom door and share their problem. Ever since they were young children, it had been that way between them.

Sitting around the table, being careful to not allow the chipped edges to scratch their arms, Bernie's family was waiting for him to speak. The children were very curious about their dad's presence at home that morning. On weekdays and Saturday mornings, while still in bed, they usually heard the jingling of his keys as he left for work. They couldn't remember the last time they saw him home on a weekday morning.

Trying to hold back his tears, Bernie grabbed his wife's hand for support, as he looked directly at Cathy and Ivan. "Last night, there was a fire at the garage, and ..." he said, stopping short, not fully knowing the best way to break the news.

Cathy asked, "Is everyone okay, Dad?"

"No..." Bernie managed to say.

Ivan asked, "Was anyone hurt, Dad?"

"Uh... Your uncle...."

"Uncle Josh? Is he going to be okay?" Cathy cried out, as tears sprang from her eyes.

"Well, let me explain. Josh stayed after hours to finish some paperwork. A few hours later, I received a phone call from the fire inspector. He was checking on all employees to account for everyone because there was a fire at the garage. I called your aunt Melanie to see if Josh had made it home, and she stated he had not and verified the fire inspector had already stopped by. She also said he had not been answering his phone."

"So, what are you saying? Is Uncle Josh okay or not?" Cathy nearly shouted, as she jerked herself up from her chair and leaned towards her father.

"Calm down, sweetie," her mother cautioned. "Let your father finish." Cathy sat down.

Bernie wiped the tears from his eyes and started again. "We don't know for sure. A body was found badly burned, and I think it was him, but there has been no word yet."

"So, we will just have to wait," Josephine said, finishing her husband's thought. "The authorities will let us know."

The children looked at each other worriedly and started to get up from the table, but their mother asked them to remain seated. Confused, and somewhat reluctant, the children retook their seats, as they attempted to wipe away the tears that were flowing steadily from their eyes.

"There is something else I want to share with you," Bernie said, looking directly at his children as he spoke.

"What is it, Dad?" Ivan asked between sobs.

"Because the shop is pretty damaged, I will be looking for another job. And until then, all of us will have to cut back on our spending and expenses."

"Will I have to cut out baseball?" Ivan asked, knowing his extracurricular activity was an added expense.

"No," Josephine answered. "Your baseball league fees have been paid for the entire season."

"Well, what about my ballet lessons?" Cathy asked, while looking down at the table, not really wanting to hear her parents' response. She feared the worst because she had often heard them discussing how they would pull extra funds together to pay the monthly bill.

"We haven't quite made a decision about that yet," Bernie said.

"I am going to try to pick up some extra hours at the diner," Josephine answered with a smile on her face, as she rubbed her fingers against her daughter's, in an attempt to reassure her.

"Mom, I can always get a job after school," Cathy began.

"Absolutely not!" Bernie yelled. "The only thing we want you to focus on is your classes. You are halfway through your junior year of high school, and you have been doing well. I don't want a job to throw your focus off now. Leave the financial aspect of this family to me and your mom."

Ignoring the rise in her father's voice, Cathy insisted, "But Dad, this job will help me with my classes and will allow me to bring in money at the same time."

"What do you mean, sweetie?" Josephine asked curiously.

"I saw a posting the other day at school for peer tutors..."

"What's a peer tutor?" Ivan cut in, as only an annoying little brother could do.

Cathy saw an opportunity to explain, in hopes of swaying her father's decision. "It's someone who tutors other students in their class. For example, I would tutor other students who are taking Algebra 2 and Chemistry 1. As I help them, I am really helping myself because that will help me study for tests and complete my homework."

"That sounds really good, Cathy," Bernie said, as he let his daughter's words sink in.

"Yeah, and it's only ten hours a week. So, I can bring in $100 a week. Will that cover my ballet lessons?" She looked at her parents quizzically.

"That will more than cover them. Each lesson is $30, and you only have one lesson a week now."

"So, can I *please* apply for the job?"

Josephine remained quiet, allowing her husband an opportunity to answer. Looking at his wife, Bernie asked her, "What do you think, Jo?"

"I think she can handle it. Let's give her a chance. It will give her experience, and it will be a great help to us." Jo knew the $100 a week would go a lot further than the ballet lessons. Cathy would be able to purchase her own clothes and treat her brother as well.

Knowing her father would agree with her mother, Cathy jumped up and hugged them both without waiting for a direct answer. Then, trying to contain her excitement, she said, "Dad, I'm sorry about the shop, and I hope Uncle Josh is okay."

"Me too, Dad," Ivan chimed in. "Is there anything I can do to help?"

Seeing his son's eagerness to help support the family, Bernie gently said, "Son, thank you for offering. I will let you know if I think of anything." Josephine patted her husband's hand, pleased with how he had responded to their children.

The Matheson family concluded their meeting with hugs and kisses all around, but something remained unsettled in all of them, as they each waited to hear the news regarding the body that was found in the fire. Cathy and Ivan prepared for a day of school. Josephine was heading to the diner to pick up her paycheck, so she could purchase groceries, and Bernie thought about his next move in life.

****

Friday afternoon, Ryan Stone got on the road in his midnight blue Mustang and headed for Vegas. He had put in a request to take that Friday off, so he could enjoy a three-day weekend to himself. He and his girlfriend Irene had been at each other's throats, and he thought he would take some time alone to think about whether or not he wanted to stay in their relationship or give it up. Irene had not appreciated how he initiated the discussion about ending their relationship. And, she had not given his phone a break after he had left her apartment late Thursday night.

That night after answering three of her calls, Ryan felt they had gotten nowhere with the shouting that took place on both ends of the phone. The next morning, his phone continued to ring incessantly, but he had decided to ignore the calls. Finally, he decided to turn the phone off altogether.

By the time Ryan had reached Vegas, he was feeling much calmer and was ready to hit the tables. Usually when he went to Vegas, Irene was by his side. That was the way it had been for the last four and a half years, but for that trip, he had to fly solo. Irene had been his lucky charm, so to speak, but that time he had to win on his own, and he felt a lucky streak was on the horizon.

After eating a nice hearty steak lunch at one of the diners on the Las Vegas strip, Ryan decided to give his luck a try. Just inside the door of the Luxor hotel, Ryan spotted a well-shaped short, blonde woman standing next to another woman who was seated at one of the dollar slots. As he walked by, unable to turn his gaze away, he got a whiff of her perfume. He continued to walk a few yards more, but something inside of him made him turn around to ask her name.

"Hey, ladies," Ryan started, as both women looked up, noticing his presence.

"Hi," the blonde spoke up, with a smile on her face, looking him up and down, as she admired his athletic attire. Ryan had decided he was going for comfort that day as he enjoyed his weekend away. He wore a Raiders football jersey, black chinos, and black Nikes.

The woman seated next to the blonde did not seem as amused by Ryan's sudden appearance. Ryan ignored the sharp look she gave him, but he could not ignore the fact that she looked rather masculine and nothing like her friend.

"Do you mind if I ask your name?" Ryan asked the blonde.

Not giving the blonde a chance to speak, the woman who was seated spoke up and said, "Hey, I'm Charlie, and my wife's name is Candy."

For a split second, Ryan looked puzzled, and the crease in his forehead deepened, as the statement ran through his mind. Then, he suddenly caught onto the relationship between the two women as the word 'wife' rattled around in his brain. He looked at them both earnestly and said, "Have a nice day, ladies." He turned around and walked away. He didn't dare look back as he chuckled.

To himself, he said, "Stay focused on the mission. You did not come out here to run after skirts. Stay focused on making your money."

For the next several hours, Ryan focused on his hands of blackjack, as he won some and lost some. By the time he decided to head back down to the MGM Grand, where he was staying, and upstairs to his room, he had a wad of cash of over $2500 in his pocket. With a smile on his face, he laid his head on the pillow and called it a night.

****

At San Francisco Memorial Hospital, Tinisha, Delores, and Rafael sat on various sides of Richard's hospital bed. The night before, his surgery had been successfully completed, and he had been transferred from ICU to a private room that Friday morning. The trio had breathed a sigh of relief and had said, "Thank you," to God.

Having her father out of the woods allowed Tinisha to be able to focus once again on the case she was presently engaged in. There was something that was disturbing her about the case, but she had not allowed herself to think about it while her father was in surgery. Now that he was out, she could mentally review her notes and begin to hone in on her next strategy to save her client from spending time in jail for a crime she did not commit. "What was it," she asked herself, "that was said just before I left court on Thursday afternoon?"

Normally, she would have gone to her office after court and recorded vital notes as she prepared for the next court session. However, with her father's emergency, the opportunity was stolen, and she was faced with recalling everything a day later.

Questioningly, she looked at Rafael as the question continued to run through her mind. Feeling her gaze, he looked up at her and said, "What is it, babe?"

"When you came into court on Thursday and I was questioning the witness, do you recall what he was saying and what I was asking him about?"

"Vaguely," he started. "I remember you asking him about a car and whether or not your client was in the car."

"That's right! Thank you! I have it now!" she exclaimed, rising from her chair and heading toward the door.

"Where are you going?" Delores asked.

"I need to call my client right away; we need to strategize for Monday's court session."

While Tinisha was in the family waiting room making her call, Delores figured it was a good time to inquire about the fire that had occurred the night before. The news channels had covered the story, but not much was being said. There was mention of arson, but no real details were given publicly.

"Son, is there any news on the person who was found last night in the fire?"

"No, Mom. But, the coroner should have news for us soon- now that the dental records have been sent over."

"Was it actually determined to be arson?"

"Yes, it was. Now, we are trying to determine the motive. A safe was uncovered, and according to Susan, the payroll clerk, everything is accounted for."

"Sounds like some type of revenge," Delores offered.

"What sounds like revenge?" Tinisha asked, walking back in and hearing her mother's comment.

"Oh, we were just discussing the Firestone fire, and your mother is playing junior sleuth again," Rafael said with a slight laugh. Rafael knew Delores liked to hear about the cases he and Tinisha worked on, so she could give her insight.

"Oh, I heard bits and pieces about that," Tinisha said absentmindedly, ignoring the latter part of his statement, as she focused on the contents of her briefcase. She was searching for the half a Snickers bar she had left in there when she spotted her laptop. She thought about how far she had fallen behind on life in general and that she should tune into her blog: "A Taste of Salisbury." It was a play on words, of course, indicating she would give people a 'taste' of legal advice. If they wanted more, they could officially request her services or that of another attorney and pay the hourly fee.

She had neglected the blog for the past few days and thought she had better take a look, knowing the questions and requests for her expertise would be backlogged. But, before she could attend to other people's legal concerns, she had to first give her paying client's case the attention it needed.

On Thursday after court, Brenda had driven home in a fog. Entering her home, she barely remembered the drive from the courthouse to her neighborhood. The brief conversation she had had with Javier was still ringing in her ears. She still could not make sense of his testimony, saying he had seen her car pulling out of the driveway.

In her heart, she knew Javier would not lie to her or about her, unless it was to protect their secret. Of all the men she had ever had a relationship with, he had been the most open with her, even more than her husband Charlie who seemed to harbor more secrets than she could count on both hands. That was one of the reasons a wedge had formed between them.

After dropping her suit jacket, overcoat, and purse on the closest chair, she walked over to the bar in the family room and poured herself a stiff drink. As she allowed the warm liquid to glide down her throat, she kicked off her three-inch patent-leather pumps and peered out the window, which provided a clear view into Javier's front yard.

At that moment, as he was pulling in, his front door opened and his daughter Marisol appeared. She was there to see to her mother's needs while her dad was at court because the in-home care nurse could not make it in that day, and the agency had not found a replacement. Marisol had two young children, but she did not often bring them to their grandparents' home because she did not want to disturb her mother's rest. Her mother had Stage 4 cancer and was not much for entertaining company, even if it was her grandchildren, who meant the world to her.

All the years Brenda and Javier had lived across the street from each other, Brenda had watched him from that very spot. She admired his good looks, dark hair, muscular-toned body, and slim physique. As she stood there watching him converse with his daughter, her mind began to reminisce about the intimate times she had shared with Javier when her relationship with Charlie had been rocky.

She and Javier had found comfort in each other's arms, as Javier was coming to grips with his wife's bout with cancer that was draining the very life from her. Although he loved his wife dearly and would never consider leaving her in her current condition, he had found the need to be with Brenda on a deeper level after developing a friendship over the past ten years. She was someone with whom he could share his innermost feelings and desires.

When he had contemplated quitting his job of twenty-three years and launching his own company, he had run the idea by Brenda, and she had completed a mock set up of his business plan and put all the numbers together for him. That gave him a solid idea about start-up costs, operating expenses, and projected profit margins. Her projections gave Javier the confidence he needed to apply for a business loan and move forward. Hence, Robles Custom Pools was birthed. His company specialized in custom pools and backyards, which included built-in BBQ grills, waterfalls, and landscaping.

As she stood reminiscing, she remembered how she loved when Javier would make tiny circles with the tip of his finger behind her ear. Oh, how she desired to feel his touch right then. The thoughts she had of him made her knees go weak. So, she thought it would be best to clear her mind and deal with reality. And the reality was- they no longer had a 'thing.'

As Javier and his daughter began to walk inside the house, he paused briefly and looked back over his shoulder towards Brenda's house. Obviously, his thoughts were on Brenda, but he knew her complete focus was on the trial and proving her innocence. As she followed his gaze, Brenda felt as though he was looking directly at her, but she knew he could not see through the custom blinds that covered the window. Shaking her head as if to shake off her thoughts and emotions, she turned away, placed her glass on the coffee table, and lay on the couch.

Marisol noticed her father's slight hesitation. "How did court go today, Dad?" she asked, wondering if that was what was on his mind.

"I'm not exactly sure, but I think Brenda is upset with me because of my testimony."

"That doesn't sound good."

"No, but I will give her some time to cool off before trying to talk to her again."

"That is probably best," Marisol said while nodding her head and following her father inside.

Before dawn on Friday morning when Brenda awoke from the cold that had enveloped her, she realized she was still in the same location she had been since she arrived home the evening before. After checking her voicemail and hearing Tinisha's message about court standing in recess until Monday, she breathed a sigh of relief. She didn't know if she could make it another day in court that week, with the prosecution attacking her character from all angles.

Wearily, she made her way upstairs to her bedroom, walked into the bathroom, showered, and went to bed. The oversized pillows and comforter felt wonderful against her skin, but she longed for the touch of her husband next to her, the body that had lay next to her and kept her warm for twenty-three years.

As Brenda tried desperately to find sleep again, her mind replayed the night her husband was fatally wounded. The court case was drudging up all the memories again. Eventually, with tears in her eyes, she found sleep and was able to experience a deep slumber.

When Brenda finally awoke that after-noon, it was to the faint sound of a ringing phone. She reached over to the charging stand to retrieve her phone but remembered she had left it downstairs. Her head felt heavy, and her legs felt like lead. She really didn't have the will to move, but with the few calls she was receiving, she knew it was neither a social call nor a bill collector. Her friends had abandoned her, and her bills were up to date. Therefore, she knew the call was about something important.

By the time she retrieved a robe to ward off the chill and had made it downstairs, the call had gone to voicemail. The caller ID showed a missed call from Tinisha. Without listening to the message, she immediately called Tinisha back.

When Tinisha answered, Brenda felt a ray of hope. The sound of Tinisha's voice always gave her a sense of comfort. When Tinisha first showed up to the jail to see Brenda, upon her request, she had taken Brenda's hand and reassured her that she would give her the best defense humanly possible. From that moment, Brenda believed she was in good hands.

"Good afternoon, Tinisha," Brenda spoke softly into the phone, remembering Tinisha's preference to be addressed by her first name.

"Good afternoon," Tinisha returned the greeting. "Brenda, is this a good time to discuss your case?"

"Of course. Would you like to meet in person?"

"Actually, that would be great."

"I would love it if you could come here. I can make lunch for us," Brenda said, noting the time on the wall clock.

"That sounds great. I'm at the hospital visiting my dad, but I will head over in about thirty minutes."

"How is he doing?"

"Well, he made it through surgery. He's resting now."

"That's wonderful."

"Thank you for asking."

"You're welcome, Tinisha. I will see you soon."

As Tinisha hung up the phone, she remembered Brenda had shared with her how uncomfortable she felt in public. Ever since her husband's murder, her arrest, and her subsequent release on bail, she thought all eyes were on her every time she was out in public. When people whispered as she walked by, she had the sensation they were talking about her and her case. Whether or not that was actually true, it was how she felt.

****

After kissing her parents goodbye, Tinisha and Rafael, both put on their coat, scarf, and gloves, walked out of the hospital together, and left in their respective vehicles, with plans to meet later for dinner. Rafael was heading back to the station to follow up on the Firestone fire and other open cases, and Tinisha was heading to Brenda's home to prepare for court on Monday.

Although Tinisha enjoyed her job, she did not particularly care for murder cases. Each time she took a murder case, she thought about how she would feel if she lost her husband suddenly without warning. Just pondering the thought caused tears to spring from her eyes. Quickly, she wiped them away and checked the mirror to see if there was any evidence of crying in her eyes. There was not, but there was a smudge in her eyeliner.

In Sunnyside, an upper class suburban area of San Francisco, she exited the freeway and pulled into a Ralph's grocery store parking lot and reapplied the eyeliner, wanting to retain a professional appearance. Although she rarely adorned herself with heavy make-up, she made a point to ensure that the make-up she did wear actually accentuated her features rather than distort them. Pleased with her look, she continued to Brenda's.

Parking in front of Brenda's Victorian-style home, Tinisha checked her face once again before exiting her powder blue Jaguar XJ8. Anticipating Tinisha's arrival, Brenda opened one side of the double front door eagerly, looking forward to having someone over but not necessarily wanting to discuss the case. Brenda had been so lonely, and the sound of her own thoughts was nearly driving her mad.

As Tinisha entered, she noticed how relaxed Brenda looked, even with a tear-stained face that she tried to hide under foundation. Brenda wore tailored black slacks with a loose-fitting silk blouse, which was much different from the Armani suit she had worn in court. Even Tinisha had dressed down a bit, wearing wool hunter green slacks, with a crème cashmere sweater under her fall/winter long cashmere coat, as she had only anticipated going to the hospital and not her client's home. *At least I'm not clad in jeans*, she thought.

From the grand foyer, Tinisha could smell the inviting aroma that wafted towards her from the kitchen. Scents of chili powder, basil, onion, and garlic filled the air. "Ummm, what smells so good?" she asked, trying to keep the atmosphere melancholy.

"Chili and fresh baked cornbread," Brenda answered.

"Sounds good," Tinisha said, as her stomach let out an audible growl. Together, Brenda and Tinisha laughed.

"Allow me to lead you this way," Brenda smiled, as she pointed toward the kitchen. When they entered the kitchen, a massive island sat in the middle with two bar stools positioned side by side. Tinisha imagined Brenda and Charlito sitting there, having breakfast or late night dessert.

In the corner of the room, a picnic-style table with benches on two adjacent sides was set for two. In the middle of the table were bowls of condiments: onions, grated cheese, sour cream, and pico de gallo. In a clear crystal pitcher was fresh-squeezed lemonade with lemon slices floating on top.

"You didn't need to go to so much trouble for me," Tinisha said.

"It was my pleasure."

With no further ado and little conversation, the two women sat down at the table and ate a hearty bowl of chili and a healthy slice of cornbread. During the meal, Tinisha reached for a glass of cold lemonade, as she experienced the sensation of fire leaping from her tongue, from the spices Brenda had included in the chili recipe.

Twenty minutes later, having satisfied themselves, it was time to get down to business. Tinisha initiated the conversation by removing her legal pad from her briefcase and picking up where court had left off on Thursday afternoon. "Brenda, I must say I am confused about Javier's testimony. I distinctly remember you telling me you were out of town with a friend. The two of you were at a cancer treatment center in Los Angeles, correct?"

Brenda nodded her head and began crying. The sudden outburst caught Tinisha off guard. But before she could express words of concern, Brenda began to apologize. "I'm so sorry," she said between sobs. "I just feel so out of sorts, with the trial, losing my best friend…" Spotting a box of

Kleenex, Tinisha reached for it and handed it to Brenda, without saying a word. Brenda took the tissue, blew her nose, and regained her composure.

"I didn't mean to upset you," Tinisha said apologetically.

"No, it's not your fault. I know we need to discuss the case. Let's move forward."

"Do you want to discuss what's upsetting you?" Tinisha asked, trying to tread lightly.

"I just miss my husband and my best friend is all. If the cancer hadn't taken Virginia, she would be by my side throughout the trial. She would not have abandoned me like…," Brenda said, as her voice trailed off.

"I'm sure that is true. It sounds like she was a really good friend," Tinisha said compassionately. After a brief pause, she continued, "Brenda, I need to understand about your car. If you were with Virginia in Los Angeles, wouldn't your car have been in Los Angeles, too? I mean, didn't you drive there, or did you fly? How could your neighbor have seen it if you weren't there? Is it possible you have the dates confused? Or, maybe Javier has the dates confused." She asked as she shuffled papers around, not seeing the confused look on Brenda's face.

Brenda had tried to jump in and answer the questions, but Tinisha was on a roll. Brenda almost felt as though she was on the witness stand, being interrogated by her own lawyer. As soon as Tinisha paused, Brenda jumped in.

"Let me explain. I did not have my car with me. My brakes had been squeaking for weeks, and my husband," she paused briefly, "suggested I take the car to our mechanic. So after work, I drove to the shop, hoping they would change my brake pads while I waited. Unfortunately, that did not happen. I was told the best they could do was possibly the next morning. I was supposed to pick up Virginia and drive to Los Angeles that night, so I called her to let her know what was going on. She suggested I leave the car and she would call a car service to pick us up. I agreed, and that's what I did."

"So, the car service came to the shop to pick you up?"

"No, one of the mechanics dropped me off at home. The car service picked up Virginia, and then, they came and got me."

"When did you pick up your car from the shop?"

"Well, because Charlie," Brenda's voice cracked, "and I both were scheduled to be out of town on Saturday, I was scheduled to pick it up on Monday after work because the shop was closed on Sundays...."

"When did you talk to Charlie about the car to make those arrangements?"

"On Friday, while I was waiting for Virginia."

"And what about getting to work Monday morning?"

"Charlie was going to drop me off Monday morning and pick me up after work to take me to the shop to retrieve my car."

"Okay. Continue. When did you finally pick up your car?"

"On Monday as scheduled, except it wasn't after work because I never made it there. It was around 11:30."

"When you picked up the car, did you notice anything strange or out of place?"

Before Brenda could answer, Tinisha jumped up and sprinted to the restroom. She had remembered passing one on the way to the kitchen. Her abrupt action caught Brenda off guard and rendered her speechless. Inside the restroom, some of the chili came flooding from her mouth and into the toilet. As she expelled her lunch, Tinisha hoped Brenda could not hear her. She didn't want Brenda to think her food had made her ill. Just as the thought passed through Tinisha's mind, she heard a knock on the bathroom door. *Oh, no*, she thought.

"Are you okay?" Brenda inquired. At that moment, the convulsions started again and more chili was released.

"Uh, I'll be right out," Tinisha said clumsily, after a few minutes. "I'm okay."

Brenda hesitated for a moment. Then, after she was sure she didn't hear any more sounds, she went back to the table. Then, she got up again to get a bottle of Tums and sat it on the table for Tinisha.

After cleaning her mouth and rinsing it out thoroughly, Tinisha made it back to the kitchen table and retook her seat, as she apologized to Brenda.

"It's okay," Brenda said. "Are you sure you are okay?"

"Yes, I'm fine. Just a little sick on the stomach."

"Would you like some ginger ale or some of these Tums?"

"Oh, no. I'm fine. Thank you." Wanting to resume the previous discussion, Tinisha re-asked her last question. "Did you notice anything strange or out of place when you picked up your car that Monday?"

"Like what? I'm sure I didn't think to look," Brenda answered, looking lost. "What are you thinking, Tinisha?"

"I'm not sure yet, but something is not right. After Javier's testimony, this car business has been bugging me. But I thought once I spoke with you and you confirmed your car was in Los Angeles, we could discredit his testimony. Now, I see that is not the case."

"What now?" Brenda asked.

"I don't know, but you can bet I will get to the bottom of it."

5

At 6:00 on Friday evening, as Rafael was just about to exit the station doors, a voice called out behind him. "Hey, Cap. A report just came in for you."

Rafael turned around and saw Detective Gonzalez standing in the corridor with a file in his hand. "Who is it from?" Rafael asked.

"It is from the coroner's office."

"Oh, it is probably the report on the burn victim from the Firestone fire," Rafael said with an anxious expression on his face.

"Oh, great. Now, maybe we can move ahead with our investigation," Gonzalez said. Rafael took the file and walked back to his office, with Gonzalez following behind. After opening the file and reviewing its contents, Rafael looked up, and with a slight shake of his head, he said, "Looks like our victim is Joshua Middleton, the owner."

"Okay, but that still leaves Ryan Stone unaccounted for," Gonzalez said.

"No one has been able to locate him yet?" Rafael inquired.

"Not yet. The fire captain left a message on his phone, but as far as I know, he has not returned the call, and he has not been located. However, one of his coworkers did say he was headed to Vegas for the weekend."

"That sounds convenient," Rafael said. "Even if that is true, it does not explain why he hasn't returned anyone's call."

"Well, what do you want to do?"

"Well, there is not much we can do. We certainly are not going to drive to Vegas on a manhunt. Let's let it sit overnight and make a decision in the morning. Meanwhile, someone needs to go over and speak with Mr. Middleton's wife and let her know what we found out."

"Okay, Milford and I will take care of it."

"Okay," Rafael said. "We will touch bases tomorrow." Feeling a small sense of accomplishment, Rafael left the station to go home and get changed, so he could take his wife out for dinner.

By the time Rafael had showered, dressed, and combed his hair, Tinisha had returned from the hospital. She had stopped in to say good night to her father and to check on his prognosis. Of course, her mother was there, sitting beside his bed. She didn't need to ask how her mother was spending her time. She knew she was knitting baby blankets for her soon-to-be grandchild.

Ever since Tinisha and Rafael had shared their good news with her parents two months ago, her mother began to imagine holding a new member of their family. At the same time, Delores knew it was not best to get in a hurry when expecting a baby, well at least not before the first trimester had passed. She recalled her own mother and grandmother being cautious about planning for unborn children. They said it was always best to have a level of certainty when it came to childbearing. Most women were out of the initial dangers of losing their unborn child when they made it past the first trimester. Tinisha was now at that stage.

When Tinisha had told her mother she was pregnant, she was already four weeks. Now, she was twelve weeks along, ending her first trimester. Saying her parents were overjoyed would be an understatement. While they had only managed to have one child, they hoped their daughter would give them multiple grandchildren. "Let's see how this first one goes," Tinisha had responded to their request.

At dinner, Tinisha could not decide what she wanted to eat. Most of the choices on the menu seemed to make her sick just thinking about eating them. Even shrimp alfredo, her all-time favorite, did not sound agreeable to her. As her husband watched her look from one page of the menu to the next and back again, he had no idea what was going on. Finally, he spoke up, "What is it, honey?"

"What do you mean?" she asked absent-mindedly.

"Well, I see you turning from one page to the next with a puzzled look on your face. Aren't you going to have your old favorite shrimp alfredo? You usually order without looking at the menu when we come here."

"No, I don't think so."

Rafael was truly puzzled. "Well, what do you have a taste for?"

"I'm not sure. What I do know is I don't see it on this menu," she said, as she placed the menu on the table.

"Do you want to go somewhere else?"

"No, maybe I'll just have a small salad."

"Are you still full from lunch?"

"No, I think my appetite is changing. That's all."

"Ah, I see the pregnancy symptoms are starting to take over," Rafael said with a smile, as he reached over and rubbed his wife's slightly growing belly. Tinisha placed her hand on top of his, following his motion across her stomach. They were really beginning to feel like the proud parents even though they still had six months until their bundle of joy arrived.

****

While Rafael was out with his wife, trying to show her a good time, Detectives Milford and Gonzalez went to visit Melanie Middleton, who was then officially a widow, to break the news to her. When they pulled up to the house, in their unmarked special model Ford, Susan, the daughter, was sitting on the porch conversing with a young man who was about her age.

By the time the two detectives had exited the vehicle and began walking up the cobble-stones that led to the front porch, Susan was standing. Wearing a long-sleeve denim shirt and a pair of Levi's with riding boots, Susan looked ultra-casual, with her blonde shoulder length curls tossed around her head. As her curiosity heightened, she stood with her arms folded, ready to address the two approaching men or for them to address her. Something inside her alerted her that their presence was concerning the fire at her father's shop, but she didn't want to be the one to verbalize it.

When the two men reached the edge of the porch, Detective Gonzalez spoke first, saying, "Good evening, ma'am."

"Good evening. Can I help you?" Susan asked somewhat reluctantly.

"We are here to see Mrs. Melanie Middleton. Is she here?"

"That's my mother. What is this regarding?" Susan asked, ignoring Detective Gonzalez's question, as she felt the tears slowly rise to her eyes from somewhere deep inside her.

"Ma'am, we need to speak directly with Mrs. Middleton. Is she here?" he repeated. Susan looked from Gonzalez to Milford, possibly looking to see if she could make any headway with him. But, he only gave her the same respectful look as Gonzalez.

Just when Susan decided to answer, the screen door swung open, and a woman in her mid-forties stepped onto the porch. "I'm Melanie Middleton. May I help you?"

"Ma'am, I am Detective Mario Gonzalez from the San Francisco Police Department," moving his arm to reveal his badge that was clipped to his belt. "And, this is Detective Steve Milford. Ma'am, would it be okay if we spoke with you inside?"

Having a full understanding of the detectives' presence on her doorstep, Melanie did not say a word. She swung the screen door open and waved her hand, ushering the detectives inside. Susan grabbed her mother's arm and walked in with her. The young man followed all of them inside and closed both the front door and screen door. Melanie fell into an armchair, and Susan sat on the arm of that chair. The young man stood next to Susan, with one hand on her shoulder. Milford looked at him and said, "I'm sorry, and you are?"

"My name is Bill McRutherford. I am Susan's fiancé."

"Mrs. Middleton and Susan, we are so sorry to inform you that the body that was found in the fire was that of Joshua Middleton." The screams that both Melanie and Susan let out were ear piercing and could be heard by the occupants in the houses on both sides and anyone passing by on the sidewalk out front. After standing and watching the emotional outbursts for a few moments, the detectives headed to the front door. Bill followed them and asked, "What now? Where's Mr. M. now? How do we get...?"

"His remains?" Milford asked.

"Um, yes."

"Have Mrs. Middleton or Susan call the coroner's office. He will be able to assist you."

"Thank you," Bill mumbled, as he opened the door, let them out, and closed the door behind them.

Later that evening, Melanie decided to call her husband's oldest and dearest friend, Bernie Matheson, to tell him of her husband's death in the fire. She would leave the other employees for Susan to call. When Bernie answered the phone, Melanie said, "Bernie, it's me, Mel."

"Mel..." Bernie let her name hang in the air.

"Yes. Two detectives came by earlier and told me Josh was the person identified from the fire." It sounded to Bernie like a question. But, he knew it was not.

"Mel, I'm so sorry that he..." his voice trailed off again. Silence hung in the air.

"I know you have to go tell Jo and the kids. We'll talk later."

"Do you need me to come by?"

"Not right now. Susan and Bill are here. Jeff will be driving over later." Jeff was

Joshua and Melanie's oldest child. He and his family lived in Oakland. Bernie knew Jeff would be heartbroken, as his sister and mother were of course, because he had a very close relationship with his father. He knew Jeff and Josh spoke every other day and visited every other weekend. Although Jeff now lived in Oakland, he and his father had still managed to carry on their father/son weekends once a month, even though Jeff was married with children. Jeff's son had come of age where he could go along also.

When Melanie's call had come in, Bernie had been walking out of the grocery store where he had picked up Stouffers lasagna, garlic bread, and fixings for a salad. Josephine was working late that evening, and all the leftovers had been eaten. Bernie wasn't much of a cook, so Josephine had left specific instructions of what to buy, so Bernie and the children could still have a healthy dinner. Starting the car and preparing to back out, Bernie suddenly shut the ignition off. The reality of the fire and the death of his boss and friend were really hitting him hard.

The tears poured down his face until he felt he had no tears left. Trying to collect himself, he restarted the car, pulled from the lot, and headed home. He thought about how he would tell Cathy and Ivan about Uncle Josh without Josephine being there. "I can't do it," he said. "I must wait for Jo." He wondered how he could pull it off because Josephine didn't get off until nine that evening. *It's not going to work,* he thought. *I can't be in the house with them and not tell them.*

By the time Bernie exited his car and entered the house, he had decided to just get it over with. He knew there would be no easy way. After Bernie placed the bags on the counter, Ivan walked into the kitchen.

"Hey, Dad. What's going on?"

"Hey, bud. Go get your sister and ask her to come in here."

Ivan yelled toward the back of the house for Cathy as he walked toward her closed bedroom door. He could hear her music escaping from under the door, so he knew she had not heard him. After knocking and giving her their father's message, they both walked to the kitchen to find Bernie seated at the kitchen table just as he had been earlier that morning.

Quietly, the children sat down and looked at their father. Bernie grabbed their hands and said, "It was your uncle that was found in the fire." Cathy and Ivan immediately grabbed one another for comfort and cried. Bernie stood up, walked around the table, and comforted both children.

Eventually, the loudness of their sobs quieted down, and both children went into Cathy's room and lay on her bed. Bernie had no more words, so he let them go. He understood their pain. Although Josh wasn't related by blood or marriage, they had always known him to be their uncle because he was their father's best friend.

Several hours later, Josephine arrived home. She was exhausted from her extended shift, but she had requested the extra hours, and she was grateful for them. After she hung her coat in the entryway closet, she slowly made her way to the kitchen. The smell of lasagna lingered in the air. A smile crossed her face because her husband had obviously done as she had asked and prepared a hearty meal for the children and himself.

When she walked into the kitchen, her smile immediately vanished. The aluminum pan of lasagna sat on top of the stove and was untouched. The garlic bread and salad were in the same condition. Quietly, she walked down the hall to the master bedroom. Bernie was lying on the bed fast asleep. She nudged him softly; he stirred. She nudged him a second time, and he lifted his head. When he saw her and she saw the look in his eyes, his tear-stained face, and loss for words, she understood.

At eleven o'clock on Saturday morning, Bernadette Folsom sat in her tiny one-bedroom apartment, tapping the tips of her fingers against the kitchen table that was worn from years and years of use. Once again, she found herself in a rut- with no job and no money. As always, she thought about calling her brother to bail her out. But that time, she thought better of it and let the idea pass by. At the same time though, she did not have an alternative plan.

A few minutes later, Bernadette lifted her head as a key turned in the doorknob. It was her on-and-off again boyfriend- if you could call him that. The sound caught her off guard because she had not seen him for at least a day and a half. Actually, she didn't quite remember what day it had been when he had stormed out. Starting to feel anxious, she dreaded what might happen next. He was very abusive- both verbally and physically, and at that moment, she just was not in the mood to deal with him and his crazy antics.

So, she quickly devised a plan. She figured if she was nice to him and if he had brought some food home or even some money, he would share with her. What she was secretly hoping was that he had scored some drugs. It had been a few days since she had had a fix, and her nerves were really feeling rattled.

James came through the door and spotted Bernadette sitting in her usual position. She felt his gaze upon her forehead, and at that moment, she realized she had not showered or even combed her hair. She wondered how off-putting she looked. She knew her very appearance could ignite his rage. He always wanted her to try to look her best even with the little she had to work with. But to her surprise, when she lifted her head, he had a smile on his face. It had been quite a while since he had looked at her fondly. As a matter fact, she couldn't remember the last time he had been pleasant with her.

When she saw the silly-looking grin on James' face, she wanted to say, "What's cooked your goose?" But instead, she said, "Hey, honey. How's your day going?" She figured it would be best not to pick a fight by asking him about his whereabouts over the last day or so.

James continued to smile but did not say a word. Instead, from behind his back, he showed her a bouquet of flowers, and in the other hand, he lifted up a white bag with red lettering on one side and grease stains coming through the bottom. At the sight of the flowers and the greasy bag, Bernadette began to grin herself. The presence of the items informed Bernadette that James had earned, borrowed, or stolen money from somewhere.

Her stomach ached from hunger, so at that moment, she could not have cared less about how he had come about the cash to purchase the food or the flowers. But as she rose from her seat, she had a flashback of the time James had hit an old homeless beggar over the head to take his cart. Then, James had ransacked the cart, looking for potential valuables to pawn or sell. That adventure netted him a whopping $78.

Erasing the thought from her mind, Bernadette kissed James lightly on the cheek, and said, "Can you place those in my purple vase?" Then, she made her way to the bathroom, took a quick shower, ran a comb through her hair, and put on clean clothes.

When she returned to the kitchen, James had placed their burgers and fries on paper plates. They both were very hungry. So quietly, they consumed their food in a rush. Before they knew it, they were done. Then, James took Bernadette's hand into his own. She flinched, fearing the worst. James ignored her familiar response and looked her in the eyes, and said, "Bern, I have some news to tell you."

"What is it?" she asked with a lowered voice, not knowing where the conversation would lead.

"Well, I was out looking for a job this morning, and I came across a delivery service that was hiring, and they actually allowed me to work today on the spot. Two of their people were out, and they needed help right away. I worked three hours this morning, and in two hours, I will go back and finish out the day. I just wanted to come home and tell you the good news while I was on my lunch break."

"That's wonderful," Bern exclaimed, not really knowing whether to believe him or not.

"Yes, but there is more," James said.

"Okay, tell me," Bernadette said feeling anxiousness rise up in her, just as it had when she had heard his key in the doorknob. She just couldn't seem to calm her nerves down even though she wanted to. She couldn't imagine he had two pieces of good news in one day.

"Next door to the delivery service, there is a clinic. There is a sign in the window saying they offer free rehabilitation services. I looked into it and spoke to a counselor just after I left work this morning, and I was able to make arrangements for you to have a free three-week detox session, if you want it."

"What does that consist of?" Bernadette asked, somewhat leery.

"Well, you would have to go into a program for three weeks," James explained.

"Is it an in-house program?"

"Yes, you would have to stay there overnight every day for three weeks. And, I really believe this is something you should do, and I will support you 100%. I know I haven't been treating you very well lately, and I apologize for that. There is no excuse for my behavior. I want us to have a brand-new start, Bern. And, I think the new job and the treatment program are just what we need. What do you think?"

"Let me think about it. Let me think about it," Bern said nervously, as she began biting her fingernails. It was a bad habit she had picked up along the way during her time of drug abuse.

"What is there to think about? Do you want to get healthy? Do you want to get better?" James insisted.

"Of course I do, but how do I know you won't just leave me while I'm inside?" Bernadette asked, sounding maniacal.

"Leave you? Bern, over the last seven years, we've been through so much together. Why would I leave you now?" James asked. Without waiting for an answer, James rose from his seat, walked over to Bernadette and hugged her, trying to reassure her he would be by her side. She wanted to believe him. She really did.

****

At noon, Ryan finally stepped out of bed, after having lain awake for thirty minutes contemplating how he would go about his day. It felt good to not have to get up and be at work at 7 AM. It also felt good to not have Irene nagging him, although he did miss her a little. However, he would never admit it if anyone asked.

After coming out of the restroom, he thought he should check his phone. He was sure he had messages from his mother, his son's mother, Irene, and anyone else who wanted to disturb his mini vacation. After turning his phone on, to his surprise, he only had four messages. Two were from Irene, and two were from numbers he did not recognize. Bypassing Irene's messages, he went straight to the others.

The first message was from Fire Captain Fitzgerald. She was informing him of the fire that had occurred at his place of employment and wanted to know his whereabouts. She stated it was strictly routine and was making sure every employee was accounted for. The next call was from the police department. The message was similar. Ryan began to get a creepy feeling moving up his spine. He felt there was more going on than they were willing to say over the phone.

Immediately, Ryan called the number to the fire station that was left on his voicemail. Once connecting with the proper authority, Ryan explained who he was and his present location. At the end of the call, fire personnel Stephanie Markowitz informed Ryan he needed to contact the San Francisco Police Department immediately. Ryan followed the instructions he was given and was immediately connected with Captain Rafael Salisbury, via Rafael's cell phone, as he was off duty, or should it be said- away from the station. A police captain is technically never off duty.

Rafael was right in the middle of an indoor basketball game, with some of his colleagues and friends, when he saw a call come in from the station. Calling a time out, Rafael grabbed a towel from a nearby bench and wiped the sweat from his face and hands before picking up his phone.

When he answered, the dispatch officer connected his call to Ryan's. Rafael and Ryan conversed briefly about the fire and Ryan's whereabouts. The identity of the victim had already been released to the news media, so Rafael didn't have any qualms about sharing the released information with Ryan. He wanted to get a sense of what Ryan knew, if anything. At the same time however, he did inform Ryan he needed to come into the station as soon as he returned to San Francisco. Ryan consented although he did not understand the purpose.

"Do you know when that will be?" Rafael inquired.

"I was planning to return tomorrow for work on Monday," Ryan replied, still very much in disbelief. "But…"

Rafael could hear the dismay in Ryan's voice and knew he was contemplating returning earlier. "Mr. Stone, to be quite frank with you, we suspect arson, and we need to question all employees in person as soon as possible."

"You think one of us had something to do with the fire?" Ryan asked, not believing his ears.

"We do not suspect anyone at this point. Our job is to find out how the fire started and if it was due to human error or intent."

Ryan did not know what to say. He had a lump in his throat the size of a golf ball. After a brief pause, he finally managed to say, "I will come to the station as soon as I am back in town, Captain Salisbury."

"I appreciate your cooperation, Mr. Stone. At the station, ask for Detective Milford. Have a good day."

After Rafael completed his call with Ryan, he called Detective Milford immediately and asked him to contact all Firestone employees and schedule a time for them to come in one by one. It was important that they jump right into questioning mode to gather as much information as possible to learn of any motives for starting the fire. Rafael also told Milford to expect a call from Ryan Stone once he returned back to

California and to also schedule a time for him to come in for questioning. Rafael hoped by questioning each employee, clues would begin to surface about why someone would want to set the building afire.

Once Rafael had given instructions to Milford, he had Milford transfer the call over to Gonzalez. Rafael instructed him to go back to Joshua's house and speak with his wife again, but that time, he would be speaking to her to find out if her husband had any enemies and if anyone would want to cause him or his business any harm.

****

While her husband was hanging out with the guys, Tinisha decided to have one of the firm's investigators check on the details of Brenda's car during the time it was in the shop. Investigator Reynolds went to the shop using the address Tinisha received from Brenda. However, when he arrived, he discovered a partially burned building with police "Do Not Enter" tape all around it. Once he returned to the office, he called Tinisha with his report.

****

After Ryan spoke with Rafael, he sat in the desk chair inside his hotel room. He could not believe what he had just heard. More frustrating, he could not believe he had not heard about the fire and the death of his boss. No one at the shop had bothered to call him.

Then, he realized he had really been out of touch by phone from trying to avoid Irene and also because he was in a casino focused on blackjack that he had not even turned on the television. The reality of Joshua's death was slowly sinking in, and Ryan felt the tears well up in his eyes. Joshua and Ryan had become fast friends when they met nine years ago at a mutual friend's birthday celebration. That meeting had led Ryan to being hired at Firestone, a few months afterward.

Quickly, Ryan packed his overnight bag, headed downstairs, and checked out of the hotel. The clerk informed him that he would still be responsible for paying for the second night stay. He didn't bother explaining his early departure. He just took the financial hit. Besides, he had an increase of $2500, so he would barely miss the money.

Once he was on the highway, the tears kept finding their way to his eyes, but he knew he had to focus on getting back safely to California. So, he tried desperately to focus as he thought about Melanie and the children, even though the children were young adults. He wondered how they were doing at that moment. Then, he began to think about the fire and how Captain Salisbury said it was probably arson. He wondered who would want to burn the shop down and who would want to hurt Josh, if that was the intent. *Well, it certainly wasn't me*, he thought.

And as far as he knew, Josh did not have any enemies. He was well known throughout their community, and most everyone who needed tires went to Firestone because Josh was a fair businessman and did not over-charge his customers. Josh had even allowed some of the repeat customers to have an account where he would allow them to take a set of tires and pay on a weekly or monthly basis until their balance was paid in full.

For as long as Ryan had known Josh, he knew Josh to have a kind heart and to genuinely care about the people he did business with. Ryan knew Josh's death had been a shock to the surrounding community.

Halfway home, Ryan pulled into a Burger King parking lot, so he could get something to eat. It was nearly three o'clock, and Ryan had not eaten all day. By then, his hunger was getting the best of him. He was so focused on Josh and the fire that he had forgotten to feed himself, but his rumbling stomach quickly reminded him.

By 6 PM, Ryan had made it home and called the police station to set up a time to talk to the detectives later that evening. While he waited, he decided to finally give Irene a call back. The first thing she said when she answered the phone was, "Honey, did you hear?" Immediately, he knew she was referring to the fire.

"Yes, I heard," Ryan answered.

"I have been calling you since late Thursday night to tell you, but I couldn't get through to you," Irene said, in a concerned tone.

"I know. I guess I should have answered my phone or at least checked my messages."

"Where are you now?" Irene inquired.

"I'm at home."

"Would it be okay if I stopped by? I don't think you should be alone right now," Irene asked, genuinely concerned about her man, knowing the relationship he had developed with Joshua over the years.

"Not right now. I am still trying to wrap my head around Josh's death. Plus, I will be headed to the police station soon."

"What for?" Irene asked quizzically.

"Well, the detectives want to question all the employees. They said they believe the fire was arson. So, I guess this is how they figure out who did it."

"Yeah, they mentioned arson on the news."

"How bad was the fire?"

"Most of the building was burned down. They showed footage on the news, but I drove by there on Friday to see the damage for myself."

At the police station, Ryan parked his Mustang in the first available spot he saw, got out, and walked through the front door. At the front counter, he identified himself and was directed to the corridor on the right and the third office on the left-hand side. As he began to make his way to the designated office, he saw Steve Rodham exiting the very office he was headed to. Steve was one of the twenty-one employees at Firestone. They greeted each other briefly and said they would connect later.

Once inside the office, Ryan answered a serious of questions about his whereabouts on Thursday night between 5 PM and 7 PM, how long he had worked at Firestone, how long he knew Josh, his working relationship with him and the other employees, and about any disgruntled employees. Ryan answered all the detective's questions, and his response regarding the disgruntled employee was, "All of the employees got along well, and the only disgruntled employee was actually an ex-employee, who had been fired about three weeks before."

"What is the person's name?" Detective Milford asked, fully expecting Ryan to say Stefan Winkleberry. That was the name that was given by two other employees during their interviews. On cue, Ryan's response aligned with the other two responses.

After Ryan left the police department, he made his way to Irene's apartment. He hoped when he arrived, she didn't rant and rave about their relationship. He just wanted to be with someone he had a close connection with during the time of his loss.

When Ryan arrived, he let himself in with his key. He heard Irene's ten-year-old son Derek playing his video games and their dog Champ howling through the patio door at a cat that was climbing the big oak tree in the back of the complex. "Hey, Ryan," Derek yelled out.

"Hey, bud. Where's your mom?"

"She went to the store. She should be right back."

Right then, Irene's daughter Chelsea walked into the living room. She took one look at Ryan and rolled her eyes. Ryan just shook his head. Derek noticed their exchange.

"What's her problem?" he asked Ryan.

Ryan shrugged his shoulders, blowing it off. Ryan had promised himself that he would never tell anyone about his interaction with Chelsea. One night after he had taken a shower, he walked into Irene's bedroom with nothing on, looking for his pajama pants.

At that moment, Chelsea was rifling through her mother's closet, looking for a dress to wear for a girls' night out, and she saw Ryan nude. Ryan ducked back into the bathroom to shield his body from Chelsea's eyes. He apologized from behind the door. Chelsea laughed and said, "No problem. Don't worry about it." Chelsea was nineteen years old and had been sexually active for a couple of years. Ryan was so embarrassed and knew he had locked the bedroom door before he went into the bathroom, so Chelsea must have let herself in, fully aware he was in the shower.

After that night, Chelsea started walking around with little to nothing on. Oftentimes, she would stand in front of Ryan as he sat on the couch and would bend over to pick up the remote from the coffee table. Sometimes, she would have on a mini skirt with nothing underneath, and he could see all she had to offer. She made lewd comments to him as if though she were trying to turn him on. Sometimes, she would have her girlfriends over in her room, and as Ryan walked by, they would be lying around in their bras and panties talking about sex. All of that took place, of course, when her mother wasn't home.

When Ryan did not take the bait of her sexual invitations, Chelsea began to have a nasty attitude with him. She never said explicitly what she wanted from him, but he knew she wanted him the same way her mother had had him. Quite frankly, he was disgusted by that idea.

He would never think of betraying her mother's trust in such a way. Chelsea, on the other hand, didn't seem to be bothered by that idea at all. Maybe she had done it before, but Ryan would not be a party to it. Chelsea's behavior was one of the reasons Ryan thought it would be best to break it off with Irene. He didn't want that to be a downfall to their relationship later. And, he most definitely did not want to be accused of abusing anyone's daughter.

7

On Sunday, Javier walked out of his front door, planning to jump into his truck and make a grocery store run. But before he made it to his truck, he had a sudden impulse to walk across the street and knock on Brenda's door. So, he did just that. Before he could completely think his plan through, Brenda opened the door. It was almost as though she was expecting him because she answered rather quickly.

But when he saw the look on her face, he knew she was expecting someone else. After all, how could she have known he was going to stop by when just a few minutes ago he didn't know himself. He began to feel as though his non-plan was a bust.

Brenda was slightly startled when she saw Javier standing there looking at her. She was actually waiting for a special delivery to come, and instead, she saw him. For a brief moment, neither of them said anything. Finally, Javier broke the ice. "How are you, Bren?"

"I'm doing okay. I guess."

"What time is court tomorrow?"

"10 AM," she said softly.

"Would you like me to be there?" Javier asked with a hopeful tone. Brenda looked utterly confused. She could not imagine what prompted him to ask that question. Seeing her bewilderment, he quickly changed the subject. "Do you have any fresh coffee?" he said, pushing his way past her.

"Uh, yeah. There is about half a pot in there."

"Oh, great," he answered, making his way to her kitchen.

"Jav, what's going on? Why are you here?"

"I just wanted to check on you. That's all," Javier said as he lifted the coffee pot, looking Brenda directly into her eyes. His gaze caught her off guard, so she turned her head away. Her reaction told him that he still moved her, just as she did him.

It had been almost two years since they had spent time together, but that did not stop Javier from what he did next. Instead of pouring a cup of coffee, Javier put the coffee pot down on the counter, turned around, and took Brenda in his arms.

Before she could object, he began kissing her. Their kiss went on for a few moments, and their embrace tightened. Before long, they were in the family room on the couch making love.

Afterward, Brenda had feelings of deep regret. Tears poured from her eyes. Javier understood her remorse. Without saying a word, he held her tenderly in his arms, as she lay on the couch and he sat upright next to her. He kissed her tenderly on the top of her head and along the sides of her face. Eventually, the tears stopped, and she embraced him as well. She laid her head on his shoulder and said, "Thank you."

"For what?"

"For loving me."

"Always," he said.

"I love you, too," she whispered, almost inaudibly.

"I know, Bren. I know. And, you don't have to worry about me. I will always be here for you. No matter what."

Although he was a married man, Brenda believed his words- that he would always be there for her- no matter what.

"Would you really come to court and support me?" Brenda asked nervously.

"Of course. You know I would be there whether you asked me to or not."

"What about Maria?" Brenda asked, concerned about Javier's wife being home alone.

"Oh, don't worry about Maria; the nurse will be with her tomorrow."

Brenda said nothing. She only nodded her head and continued to lean against Javier's chest. Bending down, Javier took Brenda's face into his hand and began to kiss her again. Before long, they were making love again. To both of them, it felt just like old times.

After Javier left, Brenda thought about her actions, and once again, the guilt flooded over her. She never imagined she could be so weak and desperate that she would succumb to her innermost needs. Finally, she admitted to herself that her actions were *not* the result of weakness or desperation. No, they were the honest reaction of a woman in love. She loved Javier like she had never loved anyone else.

The connection they had was unexplainable to someone who only saw two married people connecting in a way that violated their marriages. Even now with her husband dead and buried, their relationship was tainted by the fact that Javier was still married. And on top of that, his wife was ill and lying on her deathbed.

Until a future time, their relationship, if they actually had a relationship, would need to remain secret. For now, she would enjoy his company. At least, it would give her someone to talk to and cure her loneliness. Furthermore, in court, it would give her someone who was on her side.

About an hour later, Javier had made his grocery store run, and after taking the items into his home and putting them away, an hour after that, he went back to Brenda's house and spend the rest of the evening with her. Brenda prepared a nice hot meal for them, and they watched a couple of movies on Netflix.

In between movies, Javier felt Brenda's eyes on his back. Sure enough, when he turned around, she was looking at him. "What is it, Bren?" he asked.

"I remember longing for moments like this. You know, just to have normal days with you. I always wondered how it would be to come home to you after a long day of work."

"Maybe one day we will actually get an opportunity to find out how that would be. And speaking of work, how long has it been since you've been to work and when do you plan to go back?"

"I took off about a month before the trial started. I have never taken vacation ever since I was promoted, and I have earned six weeks' worth of vacation and even more sick days. If I am exonerated, I will go back once the trial is over."

"Brenda, it is important that you think positively. Don't say, 'if you get exonerated.' Say, 'when'."

"Okay," was Brenda's only response, as she reached her hand into the oversize bowl for more of the fresh, hot, buttery popcorn they were sharing. She didn't say it aloud, but she had her doubts.

It felt like old times for them. Except now, they did not have to leave and go to a hotel. The only concern they had was their neighbors. For the most part, everyone in their neighborhood minded their own business, but every neighborhood had busybodies.

****

After church and preparing for court the next day, Tinisha finally found time to go online to her blog "A Taste of Salisbury." As she had suspected, several messages were waiting for her. She knew she could not address all of them. So, she decided she would respond to the first three.

Janice from Los Angeles asked: I was recently involved in a car accident on the 405 freeway. A car cut into my lane and was about two inches from my bumper. Before I could slow down, I rear-ended her. I heard that the tailing driver is to blame for any rear-end accident, which is due to the assured clear distance ahead (ACDA) rule, which requires that a driver maintain an assured clear distance be-tween his vehicle and anything in front of him.

Tinisha responded: What you have stated is correct. Let's say you're following another motorist on the highway, and you're both driving at the speed limit, when the driver in front of you stops suddenly. You stand on your brakes, but you still hit the car in front of you. That's a violation of the ACDA rule. But what if you're driving along and somebody cuts out in front of you from a side street, without leaving enough room for you to stop? Or, what if somebody merges into your lane immediately in front of you without maintaining sufficient speed? These are two situations that can easily cause a rear-end collision in which you, the rear car, will generally not be held liable -- assuming you weren't speeding or violating some other traffic law. The sudden and unexpected entrance of another vehicle, pedestrian, or object into your rightful lane of travel provides some relief from the ACDA rule and accounts for the most common situation in which the driver of the rear vehicle is not liable in a rear-end collision. So, Janice, if everything was as you stated, you should be okay.

Pedro from Santa Barbara had the following concern: I live in an apartment complex that allows pets. However, I have a significant cat allergy (requiring the use of steroids). A neighbor brings her cat out into an essential hallway for playtime every night, just outside my apartment. Playtime is often late at night extending into the wee hours of the morning. She is aware of my cat allergy, but she refuses to exercise her cat in any other location. However, she lives down the hall from me and there is ample space in front of her apartment to "play." If I end up in the ER, do I have a case of personal injury?

Tinisha responded: You could sue the neighbor for negligence and may also have a claim for negligence against the land-lord. The case against the landlord may be rather weak, but you could claim the landlord was negligent for not taking corrective action to prevent the neighbor from playing with her cat in front of your apartment if the landlord had notice of your allergy to cats. There would only be one lawsuit naming both your neighbor and the landlord as defendants. Negligence is based on the failure to exercise due care to prevent foreseeable harm. Due care is that degree of care that a reasonable person would exercise under the same or similar circumstances to prevent foreseeable harm. In order to prove negligence, you would need to prove breach of the duty of due care, actual cause, and proximate cause.

Millie from North Hollywood posted the following inquiry: I received a grade I believe is unfair. Do I have the legal right to contest it?

Tinisha answered: Yes, you do have the right to contest a grade you believe to be unfair. There are five steps to initiate and resolve your grade dispute.

Step 1: Research the official college procedure for grade disputes. Every college has a different procedure. Do some research and follow the procedure specifically.

Step 2: Go up the correct ladder. No one will be pleased if you do not follow the proper chain of command. Bypassing someone will only make you look bad.

Step 3: Maintain key evidence. If order to support there was negligence or wrongdoing, you must present evidence. No one is going to accept hearsay.

Step 4: Argue the charge you can prove and win. Refrain from addressing issues you have no proof for. Focus your attention on the evidence.

Step 5: Keep the "big relationship picture" in mind. You are not attempting to destroy a relationship with your professor or the department or the school. Keep the relationship in mind.

When Tinisha finished her three responses, she had a positive vibe from being able to be a voice in her community and beyond. Thankfully, the Internet was a tool she could use to provide legal tidbits to those who desired them. As she closed her laptop for the night, she promised herself and the other site guests who had asked questions that she would catch up soon and would be back online the next day to address more of their concerns. To ensure her 'clients' patience, she offered a brief explanation of her father's illness and why she had been away from the blog site.

Thinking of her father, after tucking her laptop away, she called his hospital room. He was rapidly gaining his strength back, and he was scheduled to be released later in the week. It felt good for Tinisha to hear her father's voice. For the last few days, he had seemed like an absent force from her life. But, she felt in her soul that her dad would be back cheering with and for her soon.

8

On Monday morning, with butterflies doing somersaults in her stomach, Brenda sat at the defense table next to Tinisha. Although Brenda was nervous, Tinisha sat confidently. As they waited for Judge Hanson to enter, Brenda turned her head to quickly scan the audience. She saw Javier sitting on the bench behind her, and Virginia's daughter Monique was sitting one row behind him.

Tinisha would begin her defense after one final witness for the prosecution had testified, and Monique could possibly be called to testify that day. Tinisha had a few other witnesses scheduled to testify also.

"All rise," the bailiff called out. Everyone stood. Judge Hanson entered, wearing her black robe, took her seat at the bench, and addressed the court.

"You may be seated. We are continuing the case of the State of California v Brenda Jimenez. Mr. Hutchinson, please call your next witness," Judge Hanson said to the district attorney.

"Your honor, I call Sam Florencia to the stand." After the witness was sworn in by the bailiff, the district attorney began his line of questioning. "Please state your name and profession for the record."

"My name is Sam Florencia, and I am a taxi driver."

"Are you familiar with Javier Robles?"

"Yes, I am."

"Can you tell the court how you know him?"

"He takes my cab every few months when he goes out to the bar over on Soto Street and doesn't want to drive. I pick him up from home, and I drop him back off when he's done at the bar."

"Do you recall driving him home on the night of January 29 of last year?"

"Well, it was more like early morning on January 30."

"Please explain, Mr. Florencia."

"Well, once I pick Mr. Robles up at home and drive him to the bar, I know I am to pick him up again when the bar closes at 2 AM. But, on that particular morning I was a little late because another call for a fare had come in earlier."

"What time did you pick Mr. Robles up from the bar?"

"At 2:48 AM."

"And, what time did you drop him off at home?"

"At 3:23 AM."

"Was there anything special about this trip compared to any other trip?"

"I'm not sure what you mean."

"Did anything out of the ordinary happen to occur?"

"Not really, except when we arrived to Mr. Robles' home, a car was pulling out of the driveway across the street. Mr. Robles yelled, 'Hey, where is she going at this hour?'"

"Who was he referring to?"

"His neighbor, I guess."

"Did you see the driver?"

"No."

"What type of car was it?"

"A Mercedes."

"What color was the Mercedes?"

"Red."

"Did you see the license plate?"

"No, I did not."

"Thank you, Mr. Florencia."

"No further questions, Your Honor."

Judge Hanson nodded her head and asked, "Ms. Salisbury, cross-examination?"

"No, Your Honor."

"Mr. Hutchinson, please call your next witness."

"The prosecution rests, Your Honor."

"The prosecution has rested its case. Now, the court will hear from the defense.

Ms. Salisbury, please call your first witness," Judge Hanson ordered.

"Thank you, Your Honor. The defense calls Maurice Pullman to the stand."

As Brenda prepared herself for Maurice's testimony, she felt her confidence in her lawyer's ability to handle her defense grow stronger. Brenda realized that case was her first rodeo and hopefully her last. In contrast, Tinisha had been on this side of the courtroom for quite a while. Consequently, she had a better sense of how to prepare and what to anticipate. Brenda had always lived by the motto: "Leave it to the experts." And, there was no need to change her outlook now.

"Mr. Pullman, can you tell us your occupation?" Tinisha asked.

"I am a licensed vocational nurse," he answered.

"And Mr. Pullman, can you tell us who your employer is?"

"I work for the City of Hope."

"What is the primary focus of the City of Hope?" she asked.

"We treat cancer patients," he answered.

"And where is the City of Hope located?"

"In the city of Los Angeles."

Pointing to her client, Tinisha asked Maurice, "Have you ever seen my client, Brenda Jimenez, before?"

"Yes, ma'am. I have."

"Can you tell me the occasion?"

"I saw her several times at the clinic."

"When was the last time you recall seeing her there?"

"I saw her on Friday, January 27 through Sunday, January 29 of last year."

"And what was her reason for being at the clinic?"

"She was there to accompany a cancer patient to her monthly treatment session."

"And what is the name of the cancer patient?"

"The patient was Ms. Virginia Boswell."

"Why are you using past tense to refer to Ms. Boswell?"

"Unfortunately ma'am, Ms. Virginia succumbed to her bout with cancer in February of last year."

At that moment, Melvin Hutchinson stood and objected, saying, "Relevance, Your Honor?"

"Ms. Salisbury?" Judge Hanson queried.

"I'm getting there, Your Honor," Tinisha asserted.

"Get there quickly," said Judge Hanson.

"Yes, Your Honor," Tinisha complied.

"So, Mr. Pullman, you are here today to testify about Brenda's whereabouts because her dear friend Virginia is unable to?" Tinisha asked, re-directing her attention back to the witness.

"Yes, ma'am. Anything I can do to help."

"Did the defendant stay with the patient the entire time she was at the clinic?"

"Yes, ma'am. She did. Each time Ms. Virginia had a treatment, Ms. Brenda was there by her side the entire time."

"How can you be sure of that?"

"I was the attending nurse, and I administered all of Ms. Virginia's treatments. Every time I saw Ms. Virginia, I saw Ms. Brenda."

"For Ms. Boswell's last visit, do you recall when she and Brenda left the facility?"

"They left the clinic on Sunday evening at approximately 5 PM, just before we closed at 6 PM."

"Thank you. I have no further questions for Mr. Pullman, Your Honor."

"Cross examination?" Judge Hanson asked the D.A.

"Thank you, Your Honor. Not at this time."

"Mr. Pullman, you may step down," Judge Hanson said to Maurice. "Please call your next witness," she said to Tinisha.

"Your Honor, I call Monique Boswell to the stand." After being sworn in, Monique took a seat on the witness stand.

"Monique, I want to thank you for being here today. I know testifying in this case is not easy for you as it brings back memories of your mother."

"You're welcome," Monique said with a brief smile.

"Can you tell the court how you know the defendant Brenda Jimenez?"

"She was my mother's best friend, and she is as close to me as an aunt," Monique said in a low voice, while looking fondly at Brenda.

"Your Honor, can you direct the witness to speak a little louder? I can barely hear her responses," Hutchinson requested.

Judge Hanson looked at Monique and said, "I know testifying today may be a little difficult, but we really need you to speak louder, so everyone in the courtroom can hear you."

"I'm sorry, Your Honor," Monique said politely.

"Please continue," the judge said to Tinisha.

"Do you remember the last time your mother and Brenda spent time together?" Tinisha asked Monique.

"It was about a week before my mother died," Monique said with a light catch in her throat.

"Are you okay, Monique? Do you need a minute to collect yourself?"

"No, ma'am. I'm fine," she responded politely.

"Did Brenda make it a practice to spend time with your mother during her illness?"

"Yes, she was always there for her from the time she was diagnosed. Aunt Brenda always went to Mom's treatments with us. She never missed one. She would even come over on some weekends and cook and spend the night with us."

"Do you recall the date of your mother's last chemotherapy session?"

"It was the last weekend in January of last year."

"How can you be so sure of the date?"

"My birthday is January 30, and some of my friends wanted to take me out to celebrate on the weekend before my birthday because it fell on a Monday. Mom was scheduled for a treatment that same weekend, but she told me it was okay with her if I went out on Saturday with my friends because Aunt Brenda was planning to accompany her to the center as usual."

"And was that the treatment that was scheduled in Los Angeles?"

"Yes, it was. All her treatments were at the City of Hope."

"And how do you know Brenda actually went?"

"Because that Sunday night when they came back from Los Angeles, I was home when my mother's driver brought them both back to our house."

"What did Brenda do when they arrived back to your house?"

"She helped my mother settle into her room."

"And then what did Brenda do? Did she go home?"

"No, Aunt Brenda stayed over that night at the house because my mother was very sick. See, the chemo always caused her to vomit for at least two days following the treatment. And that weekend it was the worst ever."

"How long did Brenda stay at your house?"

"Just the one night- until Monday."

"Do you know what time she left?"

"Not exactly. When I left at eight o'clock for work, and she was already gone."

"A.m. or p.m.?"

"8 AM."

"Thank you, Ms. Boswell. Your Honor, I have no more questions for this witness."

"Cross examination from the prosecution?" Judge Hanson asked.

"Yes, Your Honor," the D. A. said, as he rose from his seat. "Ms. Boswell, you stated the defendant was at your home from Sunday evening until sometime Monday, but she was gone before 8 AM. Is that correct?"

"Yes, sir."

"And can you state your whereabouts on Sunday night?"

"I was out with friends."

"You stated in your earlier testimony that you went out Saturday night with your friends. So, are you now saying it was Sunday night and not Saturday?"

Looking directly at the prosecutor, Monique responded, "No, I went out Saturday night to celebrate with one group of friends, and I also went out Sunday night to celebrate with another group."

"What time were you out with friends on Sunday night?"

"From about 11 PM to 4 AM."

"So, if you weren't there on Sunday night for a four-hour span, how do you know the defendant was there the entire time?"

"Well, she didn't have her car. My mom's driver had picked her up at her house and drove them to L.A. Then on Sunday, he brought them directly back to my house. So, how could she have gone anywhere?"

Ignoring Monique's question, the D.A. asked his own question. "Did your mother have a car?"

"Yes."

"How do you know Mrs. Jimenez didn't drive your mother's car while you were out?"

"I had my mother's car that night. My car wasn't working properly," Monique stated, visibly annoyed with the district attorney's line of questioning.

"Do you have a written estimate or anything to prove that you were having car problems and that your car was inoperable?"

"No, I don't."

"And, did you see Mrs. Jimenez when you returned home at 4 AM?"

"No, I went directly to my room."

"And, you stated she was already gone when you left for work, correct?"

"Yes."

"So, you can't really say that Mrs. Jimenez did not leave your home that night because you were out, and there is no one else to testify about her whereabouts. Is that correct?"

"I guess I really couldn't say. But, I'm sure my mother would have vouched for her," Monique said, looking down into her hands, as she twiddled her thumbs.

"Hearsay, Your Honor. I would like that last response stricken from the record."

"The last response will be stricken. Jurors will disregard the witness' last statement. Ms. Boswell, please refrain your answers to your direct knowledge only."

"Yes, Your Honor," Monique said, with a small childlike voice.

"No more questions for this witness, Your Honor."

"You may step down," Judge Hanson instructed. "The court will stand in recess for lunch, and we will return at 1:30."

"All rise," the bailiff called out. Judge Hanson exited the courtroom, and everyone followed suit.

At the police station, Captain Salisbury and Detectives Milford and Gonzalez sat in one of the meeting rooms exchanging information from the Firestone employee interviews over lunch. "Okay, guys," Rafael started. "Let's see if we can get this sorted out. The six guys I interviewed all have alibis. They were out having drinks with some of the others."

"Yeah, I guess your six guys were out with two of the guys I interviewed. I believe they said there were ten of them total that had gone out for drinks," Milford said.

"So, that means two of your guys," Rafael said to Gonzalez, "must've been in that group of ten. Is that correct?"

"Yes, two of my guys said they were out having drinks," Gonzalez said.

"Okay, so ten are accounted for," Rafael said. "How many did you interview in total?" he asked, directing his attention back to Gonzalez.

"Seven," he answered with a mouth full of hot wings.

"Do the other five have alibis?"

"Three of them were at a Little League game."

"So were three of mine," Milford interjected, as he reached for another slice of pizza loaded with pepperoni, sausage, mushrooms, black olives, onions, and jalapeños. After taking a huge bite, one of the jalapeños caught him off guard, and he quickly reached for his can of Coke. Taking a sip, his eyes bulged.

"And the other two?" Rafael asked Gonzalez, ignoring Milford's theatrics.

"One was out with his wife, and the other, Ryan Stone, was at his girlfriend's home," he answered between laughing at Milford. Gonzalez's laugh made Rafael laugh, too.

"Okay, and you interviewed the other seven?" Rafael said directing his question to Milford, who was still trying to cool his mouth down.

"Yes. Two were at the bar, three were at the kids' game, and the other two are single and said they were home alone."

"Has that been corroborated?" Rafael asked.

"Not yet," Milford replied. "I talked to both of the neighbors on each side of their house, and not one person can vouch for them."

"That's fine. We need to pull phone records, if either of them has a landline."

"Actually, one of them does- Rocky Morris. And I've already requested the phone records. They will be sent to my email."

"Okay, great. So who is the guy that will be left without a corroborated alibi if the phone records check out for the other one?" Rafael asked.

"Allen Holmes."

"Okay, do more digging and let me know what you come up with."

"Will do," Milford consented.

"Next order of business. Did either of you get in contact with the ex-employee who was fired three weeks ago? By the way what is his name?"

"Stefan Winkleberry," Gonzalez said.

Rafael looked suspiciously at Gonzalez; then, he turned his gaze to Milford to catch his reaction, but he didn't have one. "Are you pulling my leg?" Rafael knew Gonzalez was a jokester and loved to pull pranks.

"Honest to goodness," Gonzalez said, lifting both his hands in surrender.

Still unsure of Gonzalez's sincerity, Rafael proceeded. "Did anyone check on his whereabouts for the evening of the fire?"

"Yes, he was in the hospital. He had a motorcycle accident the day before the fire and had broken his left femur."

"Okay, so we can rule him out." Rafael paused, leaned back in his chair, clasped his fingers together, and placed his hands on top of his head. "You know what?" he asked rhetorically. "We don't seem to be getting anywhere with looking in-house. Did you speak with Mrs. Middleton?" he asked Gonzalez.

"I did, and you will certainly be interested in the information she had to offer."

Rafael leaned further back in his chair with his eyes peeled on Gonzalez. Milford leaned forward, equally intent to receive the information Gonzalez had to share. But before Gonzalez could speak, there was a knock on the door.

****

During the hour and a half lunch break, Javier took Brenda to a nearby café where they shared a tuna melt to go along with a bowl of chicken noodle soup for each one of them. The soup warmed Brenda from the inside out. She was thankful for Javier's company. Sharing light conversation with him made the time go by faster. Also, he kept her mind off the district attorney's cross-examination of Monique. She didn't know what Tinisha had up her sleeve next, but someone had to testify on her behalf to solidify her actual whereabouts for that fateful Monday morning.

After lunch, Javier and Brenda walked back to the courthouse and entered the courtroom. As Brenda looked around, she saw the same familiar faces that had been in the courtroom from day one. The news crews were still present, capturing footage to air on the nightly news. And just inside the courtroom, on the first bench closest to the door, Monique sat. Brenda laid her hand lightly on Monique's shoulder; however, Monique was startled anyway from the unexpected touch.

"Oh, Aunt Bren," she said with an apologetic look. Immediately, Brenda understood the look of concern that covered Monique's face. Monique felt her testimony was damaging, and Brenda wasn't quite sure how she saw it, but she reassured Monique all was well. Brenda was confident someone else's testimony would dispel any doubt Monique's testimony may have created.

Once court resumed, Judge Hanson instructed Tinisha to call her next witness.

She called Peter Fitzgerald to the stand. Brenda recognized his face. However, at that moment, she could not remember where she had seen it before.

"Mr. Fitzgerald, please state your occupation and employer for the record."

"My name is Peter Fitzgerald, and I am a driver employed by the famous Yellow Cab Company." His statement jolted Brenda's memory, and she felt herself begin to relax some.

"Mr. Fitzgerald, keep your commentary to yourself. This is not an opportunity to advertise for your employer," Judge Hanson instructed.

"Yes, Your Honor," Peter apologized.

"Mr. Fitzgerald, are you familiar with the defendant Brenda Jimenez?" Tinisha asked.

"Yes, ma'am."

"When did you become familiar with her?"

"Well, I've only actually met her once."

"And when was that?"

"Monday, January 30 of last year."

"What was the occasion?"

"She called the cab company for a ride from a home in Nob Hill to her home in Sunnyside."

"Do you have the addresses- the one you picked her up from and the one you delivered her to?" Peter opened his travel log and flipped through the pages. Once he found Brenda's fair ticket, he recited both the pickup point and drop off.

"And what time was the pick-up?"

"The pick-up was at 4:34 AM."

"No further questions, Your Honor."

"Cross examination?"

"Yes, Your Honor. Mr. Fitzgerald, how long is the drive from the Boswell home to the Jimenez home?"

"Thirty minutes in good traffic."

"So, if I'm correct in my assumption, you delivered the defendant to her home early in the five o'clock hour? Around 5:04 or so?"

"If traffic were good that would be true. However, on that morning, there was construction on the main thoroughfare, and the trip was delayed an extra twenty minutes. So, according to my notes, I delivered Mrs. Jimenez to her home at 5:26 AM."

"And what was her demeanor when you dropped her off? Did she appear anxious?"

"No, she was tired. She told me her friend was very ill and that she had had chemotherapy the day before. Because she was keeping her friend company and making sure she was okay, she didn't get much sleep. And to make matters worse, she said she was going to go in, shower, and get ready for work."

"Did you see anyone leaving the property as you pulled up?"

"No, I did not."

"Thank you. No more questions, Your Honor."

"You may step down," Judge Hanson instructed.

****

After hearing an invitation to enter the room, where Captain Salisbury and two detectives were meeting, one of the clerks walked in with an envelope in her hand. Handing the envelope to Captain Salisbury, she said, "Here are the results of the fingerprints that were found on the can of gasoline at the Firestone shop."

"Thank you," Rafael said. After the clerk had exited the room, Rafael opened the envelope and saw two names listed. The first name was Bernie Matheson, and the second name was Allen Holmes.

"I think this definitely helps to narrow the search for possible suspects," Rafael said. "Let's do some more digging into these two."

"We are on it, boss," Gonzalez said.

"Is there anything else?" Milford asked.

"Well, yes. Gonzalez was getting ready to give us a bit of information."

"That's right," Milford agreed. "What's up, man? What's going on?"

"Yes, please tell us," Rafael encouraged.

"Well, when I went to speak to Joshua's wife, she told me that several months ago when Joshua decided to expand his business, by adding extra footage to the existing structure, he couldn't get a loan from the bank, so he had to take out a hard money loan."

"Wait. What do you mean by a hard money loan?" Rafael asked. "You mean with a high interest lender or a loan shark?"

"A loan shark," Gonzalez said matter-of-factly.

"Okay. Go on," Rafael encouraged.

"Well, the balance of the loan had come due, and Joshua didn't have all the money to pay off the loan."

"I'm starting to get the picture," Rafael said, and Milford just nodded his head in agreement. "What is the name of this loan shark?" he asked. Then, without waiting for a response, he said, "Oh, no. Let me guess, Tommy Caruso?"

"Right, boss."

"I'll try to get in contact with him today," Rafael said as he stood up. "He should be in his office over on Main Street."

Tommy Caruso was well known in the community as the 'go-to' guy if the bank denied a loan. As long as the loan was paid back on time, with the required interest, the borrower would have no issues. However, if a loan payment lapsed, there were consequences and repercussions. And, based on past 'rumors,' no one wanted to fall out of Tommy's good graces.

"Will there be anything else, boss?" Gonzalez asked.

"No, that's all for now," Rafael said, dismissing the two. "Thank you guys for good work," Rafael added, as the two detectives walked out the door, taking the rest of the pizza and hot wings back to their desks.

****

After the taxi driver stepped down from the stand, Judge Hanson asked Tinisha to call her next witness. Tinisha looked up at the judge and asked, "May I approach the bench, Your Honor?"

Judge Hanson beckoned for both lawyers to come to the bench. Once they had reached the bench, the judge covered the microphone before Tinisha spoke. Tinisha, speaking softly, said, "Your Honor, I need to request a continuance. I just learned that the body shop my client had her car being serviced at has burned down and the records are no longer available. I am attempting to locate the mechanics who were on duty when her car was taken to the shop."

"Do you mean the Firestone fire that happened a few days ago?" Judge Hanson inquired with raised eyebrows.

"Yes, Your Honor."

"Any objections?" Judge Hanson asked the district attorney.

"No, Your Honor."

Judge Hanson motioned to the lawyers to return back to their tables. Uncovering the microphone, Judge Hanson said, "Court will remain in recess until tomorrow morning at 10 AM. Court is adjourned."

James had begun his Monday by sitting on the bed, as he watched Bernadette pack her worn suitcase. He wished he had money to buy her a new one, so she could go to the treatment center with a little style. But at least he was able to buy her a couple new outfits, so she wouldn't look haggard and worn with the clothes she had. He enjoyed the smile she had on her face. He couldn't remember the last time he had seen it. Well, before he brought her flowers on Saturday morning, that is.

For the past few months, she had been down in the dumps and was trying to kick her drug habit all by herself, and frankly, she was getting nowhere. When he first brought up the idea about the treatment center on

Saturday morning, Bernadette had been a little reluctant. But over the course of the weekend, James had been able to talk her into it and reassure her that he would not leave her while she was in the process of recovery.

For the past couple of days, James' position as a courier for the delivery company had worked out well for him. He was able to work a full shift on Saturday and a double shift on Sunday. In just two days, he had brought in over $300. With the money he had earned, he was able to put some of it away for the next month's rent. But he wasn't actually sure if he was going to pay rent or give a notice to the apartment manager.

He and Bernadette had lived in that small rundown apartment for much too long, and it was his desire to move her into a more positive environment, one that was not in a community infested with drugs. But, he had not spoken his desires to Bernadette. He did not want to get her hopes up just in case he was not able to pull it off. But, he was ready to do some searching right after he dropped her off at the center and finished his shift for the day.

He had seen several apartment buildings that looked very promising from the outside, as he was making his deliveries. So, he would start with some of those and see if he could work out something with one of the managers. He thought it would be a fantastic idea to take Bernadette home to a new apartment when she was starting her new life- clean and free from drugs.

When James returned to work, he had a level of excitement that his boss had never seen in him in the few short days he had known him.

"What's going on with you?" Lenny asked. "You seem excited about something."

"I am. Remember I mentioned to you about my girlfriend and her problem?"

"Yes."

"Well, I was thinking it would be awe-some to find an apartment during the three weeks she's in the program and move her into it once she is released."

"Wow, that sounds like an awesome idea. Hey, you know there may be something I can do to help you out."

"Really? That would be awesome."

"Yes, my brother-in-law is an apartment manager. He manages several buildings in a few different neighborhoods. Is there any-where specific you want to live?"

"Somewhere close to here would be nice, seeing that I don't have a car. That will make it easier to get to work. Right now, I'm riding the bus, and it takes me thirty minutes to get here."

"Let me see what I can do, and I'll get back to you by the time you finish your shift this evening."

"Thanks, Lenny. I don't know how thank you."

"Well, don't thank me yet. Let me see what Dale has to say. I know he's going to ask one specific question though."

"Yeah, what is it?"

"How much can you put down? Generally, they ask for first and last month's rent, along with a security deposit."

"Well, seeing that I just started working," James said with a smile, "it may take me more than three weeks to come up with that kind of money."

"Yeah, I hear you. Let me talk to Dale and see what he can do."

"Thanks, Lenny. I appreciate it. Even if it doesn't work out, I appreciate the thought." With a smile still spread across his face, James set off to deliver the next set of packages the office manager had set aside for him.

****

When Tinisha left court for the day, she headed over to San Francisco Memorial Hospital to check on her dad. So far, he had been recovering well after his triple bypass surgery on Thursday. His doctor stated he would need to stay in the hospital to the end of the week. He wanted to ensure that the new heart valves were working well.

When Tinisha arrived to her dad's hospital room door, she was greeted by some of the church members who had come to pay him a visit. There were many more plants, bouquets of flowers, and balloons all around the room than there had been the last time she had visited. Anyone who passed by in the hallway could tell Pastor Oglebee was well loved and respected. When all the guests had departed, Delores sat in a chair chuckling to herself. Tinisha looked at her dad; her dad looked at her, and they both looked at Delores.

"What's so funny, sweetheart?" Richard asked.

"Oh, I'm just laughing at these floozies we have in our church. Some of them will never get the message until you are cold in the ground," she said, as she laughed loudly. Tinisha knew exactly what her mother was talking about. Over the years, she had seen women throw themselves at her father with no mercy. Richard's eyes went toward the ceiling and said, "Love, you know there is only one woman who was meant for me."

"Honey, you don't need to explain. I am not concerned in the least. It is just so hilarious to me that it is still going on after all this time. I could write a book about the scandalous women that come around year after year. A book that would warn all other first ladies or co-pastors what their husbands have to deal with."

"But you wouldn't name names would you, Mom?" Tinisha asked.

"Oh, no! Of course not, honey. I would just call them floozy number one, floozy number two, and so on," Delores said laughing heartily. Her laughter was so contagious that her husband began to laugh, too. But then Delores stood up, put her hand on her husband's chest and said, "Now take it easy."

"Laughter is good for the soul," Richard said, objecting to her loving rebuke.

"Yes, but it is not good for your stitches."

"Well, she has a point there," Tinisha said, holding back her own laughter.

"You two are bad," Delores said as she retook her seat, while shaking her head and grinning from ear to ear.

After leaving the hospital, Tinisha went to Panda Express on her way home to pick up dinner. Her favorite dish was Black Pepper Chicken; however, Rafael's favorite was Kung Pau Chicken. So, she got a little bit of both along with Chow Mein and Shrimp Fried Rice. When she made it home, Rafael was already there and had made himself comfortable.

After depositing the items on the kitchen counter, she walked back into the family room and said, "Hey, honey. I need to ask you a question."

"Okay," he said, as he stood and kissed her and slid his arms around her waist, rubbed her slowly growing belly. "What is it?" he asked.

"I just found out that my client's car was at the Firestone on Billings Road being serviced the same weekend her husband was killed."

"Okay," Rafael said, still waiting for the question.

"Well, I sent an investigator to find out which of the mechanics were on duty that weekend and to find out if they noticed any-thing strange with Brenda's car. But because there was a fire, all the records were destroyed. I'm assuming. So, I don't know what to do. Do you have any ideas?"

Rafael said, "What you might want to do is check with the bookkeeper/payroll clerk, the owner's daughter. She may be able to help you out."

"Oh, that sounds like a great idea. Do you happen to have her contact information?"

"Absolutely. Let me get it for you," Rafael said, as he released his wife from his bear hug and walked over to his spiral pad where he kept notes on the Firestone case. He passed the information to his wife, and the two enjoyed their supper.

Afterward, Tinisha contacted Susan right away. To her disappointment, she reached Susan's voicemail. So, with no other viable choice, Tinisha left her a message. But before Tinisha could put her phone down on the nightstand, it rang. Immediately, she recognized the number as the number she had just dialed.

"Hello, Susan?" Tinisha asked.

"Yes, this is Susan. Who is this please?" Obviously, she had not listened to the message that quickly and had no idea who was calling her.

"My name is Tinisha Salisbury, and I am the attorney for one of your clients at the Firestone shop. During the weekend that her car was being serviced, unfortunately her husband was murdered, and she is now on trial. So, I would like to verify with you that her car was indeed in the shop. I do understand that your business suffered a fire, and I'm sorry to hear about the loss of your father."

"Thank you," Susan said softly.

"Were all client records destroyed in the fire?"

"Fortunately, I have the customer record logs saved on my laptop, and I had my laptop with me at the time of the fire. What is the name of the client?"

"Her name is Brenda Jimenez."

"Okay, give me just a moment, and I will look up her log. A subpoena for personal records is required, but this case has made national news, and I recognize your name and voice from television, so I'm going to give you the requested information."

"Thank you so very much."

"You're absolutely welcome." After a brief silence, Susan came back on the line and said, "Yes, I have her log here. Exactly what date are you looking for?"

"It was the last weekend in January of last year- uh, January 27," Tinisha said, as she did her happy dance.

"Yes, I have the invoice here. She dropped her car off on the 27th and picked it up on Monday the 30th."

"Oh, that is great! Can you email me a copy of it?"

"Sure, no problem. What is your email address?"

After providing her email address, Tinisha thanked Susan for her kindness and for calling her directly back. When she got off the phone, she checked her email and the invoice was already there. It was the ammunition she needed for court the next day.

****

Once James finished all the scheduled deliveries, he stopped back by the office to give his report to Lenny before heading home. Lenny was in his office, and the office manager, Marissa was seated at her desk in the outer office.

"Marissa, is Lenny still around? I need to give him my report."

"James, you know you can always leave your report in the report drop box, unless there was a problem with a delivery."

"Oh, no. No problem at all. I actually just wanted to follow up on another conversation Lenny and I were having earlier."

"Well, why didn't you just say so?" Marissa said teasingly.

James did not respond. He just stood there with an embarrassed look on his face.

To smooth things over, Marissa said, "Let me see if he is available." James simply nodded. He did not know Marissa well, so he did not know if she was joking or serious. So, he thought it would be best to say nothing.

When Marissa finished her call, she gave permission for James to go back into Lenny's office. Once inside, Lenny asked him to have a seat. Following instructions, James sat in the chair directly across from Lenny. Before James could ask the question that was burning inside him, Lenny spoke up.

"I spoke to Dale, my brother-in-law, and he has some vacancies in a couple of the apartment buildings that he manages. He said whenever you are ready, feel free to stop in to take a look and give the on-site manager his name. Here is a list of the addresses," he said, handing James a sheet of paper with addresses and phone numbers highlighted. Dale's number was written across the top. James thanked Lenny and left on cloud nine. He finally felt like things were changing for the better! For both he and Bernadette!

10

As soon as James received the list of apartments and addresses, he walked out of Lenny's office and called Dale to thank him for sending the list over. Dale answered right away as he was anticipating James' call. There were two apartment buildings relatively close to the courier service, but James would need to get there quickly because the on-site manager of each building only had one hour to show the property prior to closing time. James had desired to stop in and see Bernadette before he left the area; at the same time, he wanted to give her an opportunity to settle in because it was only her first day.

So, off he headed to the first apartment complex- Ashton Lane Townhouses. When he arrived, Teresa showed him around the complex. The building was very nice, and there was even a playground, complete with swing sets and jungle gyms, right in the center of the parking lot, where the children who live there could play safely, without leaving the complex. There were some furnished apartments as well as unfurnished ones. James thought a furnished apartment would be a nice idea. That way, he and Bernadette would not be required to take their old furniture with them. Also, they would not be required to buy new furniture right away. But the price of the one-bedroom apartment was so exorbitant, James could not even consider it.

Disappointedly, James left and headed to the next apartment complex- Willow Brook Springs. He only had thirty minutes to get there and see the apartment. When James arrived inside the manager's office, there was a couple filling out a rental application. He checked his watch and saw time was drifting away. Sheila, the on-site manager, noticed his anxiety and remembered speaking to him just minutes before, so as the couple was busy with the application, she walked over and told him, "I will be with you in just a moment. Don't worry about the time."

Feeling relieved, James took a seat in the waiting area. After the couple had completed the paperwork and paid their security deposit, Sheila took James on a tour of the property. That property was not as nice as the property he had seen before, but it had so much to offer. There was an on-site workout room, and each unit had its own laundry facility. There were two parking stalls assigned to each unit not that it mattered at the moment, seeing that neither he nor Bernadette had an operable vehicle. There was only one one-bedroom unit that would be coming available in the next couple of weeks, towards the middle of the month.

The price was right, and James was very much interested. It was only a few miles from the courier service and Bern's treatment center. James would be able to make it to work by bus in only ten or twelve minutes.

The only problem with acquiring the apartment that he could foresee was the requirement of first month and security deposit. He needed to calculate how much money he could make over the next couple weeks in order to get the money he needed. Later that night when he made it home, after doing his calculations, he found out he would be short $450, unless he worked more hours.

He thought of calling Bern's brother to see if there was something they could cook up very quickly to get the money in the next two weeks. But he and Bern had decided they were going straight- no shenanigans and no drugs. *But, I could do this just one last time*, he tried to reason with himself. But as the saying goes, "Is there really a last time?"

Thinking better of placing himself in a no-win situation, James took a deep breath and changed his thought pattern, as he arrived home. "I will just talk to Lenny to see if I can put in a little overtime over the next couple weeks," he said aloud to himself. "He was so considerate to talk to his brother-in-law on my behalf. I really don't want to push it by asking too much. I just started working there. I don't want to blow it." *Or, maybe I could work something out with Dale,* he thought, finishing his reasoning in his head.

Calming his anxiety, he made himself a can of beef stew, which left a lot to be desired. As he ate, he realized he was going to miss Bernadette for more than one reason, but he would have to make the best of it. If she could sacrifice for three weeks, so could he. After his meal, he called it a night. He decided it would be best to let his ideas simmer and revisit them the next morning.

****

Rafael left the police station on a manhunt, on a search for the popular loan shark Tommy Caruso. His first stop was Caruso's office on Main Street. Unfortunately, when Rafael arrived, the offices were closed for the day. The posted business hours were 8 AM to 5 PM, and at that point, it was 5:30 PM.

Rafael placed a call to the bar over on Burgos Avenue. Mel, the bartender, answered the phone, and Rafael inquired about Caruso's presence in the bar. Mel confirmed, and Rafael ended the call, to make his way there.

When Rafael made it inside the bar, he spotted Caruso right away sitting at one of the back tables with a group of his cronies. Weaving through the tables, Rafael hoped to reach Caruso before he was spotted. But before he made it to Caruso's table, sitting at another table was one of the police station clerks, and she called out his name. That caught the attention of nearly everyone in the near vicinity.

Caruso heard Captain Salisbury's name, looked up, and their eyes met. Caruso knew Rafael was there to see him, but of course, he didn't know the reason for the personal visit. To appear cordial and unfazed, he stood and said, "Captain."

"Mr. Caruso, may I have a word with you?" Rafael asked.

"Of course, Captain." Then to the men who were seated with him, Caruso said, "Gentlemen, if you don't mind excusing us for just a moment." Without saying a word, the three men slid their chairs back, stood, nodded to the captain, and walked away.

"Please, have a seat, Captain."

"Mr. Caruso, I will not take much of your time. But, I do have a few questions that I must ask you regarding Joshua Middleton."

Without waiting to be asked, Caruso began speaking. "Captain, I didn't have anything to do with the fire at Firestone if that's what this is about."

"Well, first I want to know if the information I received about him having a hard money loan out with you is accurate."

"Yes, he did have a loan out with me. For exactly $90,000."

"Why did he need the money?"

"He said he wanted to add onto the existing structure at the shop."

"And is that what he did as far as you know?"

"Well, I did see more bays at the shop, but I can't say if that's what the entire $90,000 went to or not. But that was really not my concern. You can understand that, right?"

"Of course," Rafael said. "Did Josh pay you all the money back he had borrowed?"

"He had paid $65,000 of the loan back."

"Okay, so he had a balance of $25,000. Correct?"

"No. He had a balance of $35,000. There was a $10,000 loan fee."

"When was his next payment due?"

"It had come due a few days before the fire."

Rafael lifted his eyes and looked directly at Caruso. "Did you speak to Joshua about it?"

"No, he had called the day before the due date and asked for an extension, which I granted. He had made all his other payments on time, so I figured what would be the harm."

"How generous of you," Rafael said with a touch of sarcasm.

"I try to please my public."

"And how do you plan to collect the remaining balance now?"

"Well, seeing that he died, the debt died with him. That has been my longstanding policy."

"Did you have anything to do with his death?"

"Absolutely not."

"Do you have an alibi for Thursday, January 23 from 5-7 PM?"

"As a matter of fact I do. I was in Lake Tahoe. And, I just came back to town last night."

"Can anyone verify your alibi?"

"Yes, my wife was with me."

"And, at which hotel did you stay?"

"We weren't at a hotel. We have property up there."

"Okay, is there anyone else who can vouch for your whereabouts?"

"Well, I'm sure. We had dinner at several of the restaurants, and we did some shopping in town. I'm sure I can get credit card receipts from my wife for the stores she shopped at showing the date and time. Will that suffice, Captain Salisbury?"

"Sure, have her bring them to the station and copies will be made and the originals returned to her," he said standing and preparing to leave. Without waiting for an objection to his last statement, he reached across the table, shook Caruso's hand, turned around, and walked through the bar and out the front door.

****

After Javier returned home from court, he spent some time sitting with Maria. However, she was asleep most of the time. Those days were filled with a lot of pain for her, and the in-home care nurse kept her sedated with the medications that were prescribed by her primary physician. From what the doctor had said, Maria didn't have much time left, and they were just trying to make her as comfortable as possible.

As Javier sat there next to his wife's bed, he could not help but to think about the woman who lived across the street who had his heart. He and his wife had lived good years together, raised their children, and had built so many memories. Now, Brenda was taking over his world, just as she had done before. He knew that was one of the reasons she had to back away from him. He had been consumed by her and had wanted to see her all the time.

When his mind cleared, he realized the chapters with Maria were not over yet. As he sat, he felt so torn. He knew it would not be best to leave his wife at that moment. He would be completely devastated if anything happened to her when he wasn't around. So he sat, and he held her hand.

Later that night though, he went into the living room and called Brenda. He really wanted to be there with her, but he knew that night was not the best night for a visit. He did look forward to seeing her in court in the morning though. So, at that moment, hearing her voice would have to do.

The next morning, the nurse came at 6:30 AM to relieve Javier. Normally, at that time, he began showering and preparing for his day. But on that day, he was prepared to walk out the door. Once the nurse came in, set up, and had everything she needed, Javier quickly departed.

He checked the street to make sure no one was leaving home to head to work or to drop off children at school. Then, he walked directly across the street and entered Brenda's house with the key she had given him during his last visit. They both thought it would be a good idea if he just walked in quickly and didn't have to stand there possibly being noticed by any of their neighbors while he waited for her to answer.

Prior to going over, Javier had sent her a text just before he left home, so he would not startle her by suddenly appearing. He was not sure if she had received his text or not because he heard the shower running as he entered her home and approached the staircase. Plus, he had not received a reply. He called out her name to make her aware of his presence. After the ordeal she suffered with the murder of her husband, he did not want to cause her any alarm.

After calling out to her, from halfway up the staircase, she responded by saying, "I'm in here. I'm in the shower." Continuing up the stairs, Javier entered Brenda's bedroom, undressing as he went. By the time he made it to her bathroom door, he was completely nude. He joined her in the shower.

Afterwards, they spent a couple hours together before preparing for court. Brenda was due to take the stand, and she was feeling a little unnerved by it all. After a little coaxing and reassuring, Javier was able to calm her nerves- at least for a little- with his gentle touch.

For those precious moments, he was able to take her mind off everything, except them and the love they shared. Each time she smiled, his heart melted a little more.

11

One of the requirements of Bernadette's recovery program was to participate in group therapy. Group therapy consisted of joining a group of the same sex and listening to testimonies and sharing your own. That activity was designed to get the participants to understand what led them to become abusers, so they would know how to avoid falling into the same condition again. As Bernadette listened to the other women share stories of their childhood, she began to have flashbacks of her own. But, she wasn't yet ready to open up and share.

That night, after listening to one story after the other, she had nightmares about her childhood experiences. The nightmares led her to share a portion of her story during Tuesday's session. After three women had spoken, Bernadette raised her hand and introduced herself again and began to share an account that had traumatized her for many years of her life.

One afternoon, when she was seven years old, her father returned home from a drinking binge and stormed into the house looking for Bernadette's mother.

Unfortunately, Bernadette was familiar with her father's bouts of rage, so she knew to stay out of his way. When he barged through the front door, she hid in the hallway closet. She closed the door just in time for him to walk by without noticing her. Once he reached the bedroom he shared with his wife, Bernadette heard a scuffle begin. All she could do to block out the sounds of her mother's screams was to cover her ears and sing softly to herself. She had found singing to be a good coping mechanism for horrific moments like that.

Finally, the screams and the banging stopped; then, the front door slammed shut. When she finally had the nerve to open the closet door, she inched it open little by little. She tiptoed into her mother's bedroom only to find her mother's nude body in a bloody heap on the floor. Bernadette screamed and screamed until her brother came from his hiding place to see what the commotion was about. As Bernadette continued to scream and cry over their mother's body, her brother dialed 911. That night, their mother died in the hospital, from severe blunt force trauma to her skull.

After her mother's death, her father was arrested and subsequently jailed. Bernadette and her brother went through many years of therapy and were moved from one foster home to another. Eventually, despite her childhood, she grew up to be a strong young woman who went to college, earned her degree, and graduated with honors. However, she ran into some problems during her employment, which led her quickly onto a downward spiral because of the brokenness that lurked underneath her strong exterior.

Hopefully, the stent of therapy Bernadette was presently undertaking would be just what she needed to move forward in her life and free herself from drugs and the bout of depression she had been suffering.

****

On Tuesday, at 9:30 AM, Tinisha met with Brenda in one of the lawyer/client meeting rooms at the courthouse. Brenda was experiencing anxiety about taking the stand that morning, but Tinisha reassured her that she only had to answer the questions truthfully, and Tinisha, as her lawyer, would handle the rest.

Twenty minutes later, both women left the meeting room to make their way to the designated courtroom they had been in for over a week. But before they could make it safely through the courtroom doors, Bree Wilkerson, one of the Channel 7 news anchors, interrupted their walk. Pointing the microphone in Brenda's face, Bree asked,

"Mrs. Jimenez, did you kill your husband Charlito Jimenez?"

Before Brenda could even think about answering, Tinisha moved in front of the microphone and answered the question for her. "She has no comment," Tinisha asserted. Bree attempted to ask a second question, but Tinisha firmly stated, "We are headed into court right now, as you very well know, so we cannot take any questions at this time."

A few minutes later, after brushing past an additional group of reporters, Tinisha and Brenda were seated at the defendant's table in the courtroom. Judge Hanson entered shortly after and went through the formalities of starting court and directed Tinisha to call her first witness of the day.

"I call Susan Middleton to the stand."

Once Susan was sworn in and had taken her seat on the witness stand, Tinisha began her line of questioning. "Please state your name and occupation for the record."

"My name is Susan Marie Middleton, and I am the payroll clerk for Firestone tires located on Billings Road."

"Ms. Middleton, are you familiar with the defendant Mrs. Brenda Jimenez?"

"Yes, I am."

"In what capacity do you know her?"

"She and her husband Charlie are our customers... were our customers... I'm sorry. They are our customers... I'm sorry... She is a customer of Firestone Tire." Susan was so flustered; she dropped her head and began to weep as she thought about how neither her father nor Charlie was alive- not that she knew Charlie well, but he had been a long-time client.

"And do you know the last time she had her vehicle serviced at Firestone?"

"According to her service log, she came in November of last year for a service "A," which is an oil change."

"And while you're looking at her service log, do you see a date for January of last year?"

"Yes, I do."

"What date did she take her car in to be serviced?"

"She brought her car in on Friday, January 27 at 5:13 PM."

"And was her car repaired the same day?"

"No, her car was not repaired until late Saturday, January 28."

"When was the car finally picked up?"

"She picked up the car at 11:34 AM on Monday morning."

"So, her car was parked at your facility from Friday evening when she dropped it off until she picked it up Monday morning?"

"According to our records, yes."

"Thank you, Ms. Middleton, and again my condolences. I have no further questions, Your Honor."

"Cross-examination, Mr. Hutchinson?"

"Thank you, Your Honor," the district attorney said, as he rose from his seat. He was dressed in a three-piece black pinstripe suit, which was much different from the basic colored suits he had previously been wearing. *Maybe he thinks he is doing well and wants to look the part*, Tinisha thought as she watched him walk towards Susan.

"Ms. Middleton, my condolences as well. You stated the defendant's car was at the shop the entire time from Friday to Monday. Is that correct?"

"Yes."

"And was the car parked inside the garage or outside the garage?"

"The car would have been parked outside the garage unless it was being worked on."

"And when exactly were the brakes repaired on the car?"

"The brakes were repaired on Saturday afternoon at 3:28 PM."

"And how long would you say it takes to repair brakes?"

"Well, it depends on the job. For Mrs. Jimenez's car, she had brake pads and rotors installed, so it would have taken approximately two hours."

"So, her car would have been completed at approximately 5:28 PM. Correct?"

"Uh, yes. That's correct," Susan said as she glanced at the log.

"So from about six in the evening on Saturday to some time Monday morning, the car was parked outside of the garage, correct?"

"Yes, that would be correct."

"Ms. Middleton, please explain to the court how you know for certain that the defendant's car did not leave the property of Firestone Tire from the time it was repaired to the time she picked it up on Monday afternoon."

"I'm not sure what you mean."

"How do you know the defendant did not come to the shop, remove her car, and return it anytime during the time it was parked?"

"Well, if she had done so, any one of the mechanics or staff would have seen her. And if she picked it up before Monday, why would she bring it back and then come back again on Monday to pick it up? I'm not sure I follow your line of questioning," Susan said very confusedly.

"What about after hours? Wouldn't it be just as easy for a car owner to pick up his or her vehicle anytime he or she wanted to?"

"Not necessarily because we have the keys locked away in the office. The only way someone could retrieve his or her car is to get the keys from the office."

"What if the person had a spare key?"

"Again someone would have seen him or her drive away with the car."

"What about after hours? Couldn't a person simply walk onto the parking lot and remove his or her vehicle?"

"No, they could not because at the end of business hours, the gates are locked, and no one except employees could gain entrance to the facility."

"Your Honor, I'd like to introduce Exhibit A into evidence," Mr. Hutchison said while showing the judge a photograph. Judge Hanson looked quickly at the photograph and nodded her head. Then, Mr. Hutchinson nodded to the technician who immediately displayed the image on the monitor for everyone in the courtroom to view. The image showed Firestone Tire badly burned. When Susan caught sight of the image, she caught her breath, and tears immediately spring from her eyes.

Right away, Mr. Hutchinson began to apologize profusely regarding his absent-mindedness about the delicacy of the situation surrounding her father's death. Before he could continue his apology, Judge Hanson stepped in to soothe the situation.

"Ms. Middleton, do you need a moment to collect yourself?" Judge Hanson asked sympathetically.

"I'd rather get finished as quickly as I can," Susan responded.

"Please continue, Mr. Hutchinson," Judge Hanson instructed.

"Ms. Middleton, can you explain what this is an image of?"

"Yes, it is an image of my family's business: Firestone Tire."

"And Ms. Middleton, do you see any gates around the perimeter of the property?"

"No, I do not."

"But a few minutes ago, you said the car was locked inside the gates at the end of business each day. Isn't that correct?"

"Yes, I did."

"So, can you explain why we don't see any gates in this picture?"

"Yes, the gates were taken down a few months ago when my father began construction to expand the existing structure."

"So, are you trying to say prior to a few months ago there were gates around the perimeter?"

"Yes, that is exactly what I'm trying to say," Susan said with an annoyed tone in her voice.

Ignoring Susan's apparent frustration, Hutchinson continued his probing. "To be specific, were the gates around the perimeter on January 27 through the 30th of last year?"

"Yes, the gates were there during that time last year."

"No further questions, Your Honor," Melvin said, sounding like his ego was a little deflated.

"Re-approach, Ms. Salisbury?"

"Yes, Your Honor. Thank you."

"Ms. Middleton, you stated that a car owner cannot simply walk in and remove a car from the lot, correct?"

"Yes, that is correct."

"What about an employee?"

"I'm sorry- what do you mean by that?"

"At night, when the gates are locked, which employees have access to the gate?"

"Only employees who have been with us for a number of years, who are responsible for opening and closing the business, in addition to my father and myself."

"So, you are saying that Mrs. Jimenez's car could have been removed from the lot, but it would not be very likely that she removed the car; however, employees did have access to the gate?"

"I don't think any of our employees would remove anyone's car."

"Ms. Middleton, can you please answer the question that I asked you? As you stated, employees have keys to the gate granting them access to any car at any given time, correct or not?"

"I guess I would have to say that is correct," Susan stated reluctantly.

"Thank you. Your Honor, no further questions." Having said that, Tinisha finally felt she had made some headway in the case to proving her client's innocence. She could see from the look on the onlookers' faces that they had the same feeling as well as she turned away from Susan at the witness stand and headed back to her seat. Brenda could not keep from smiling as she felt a ray of hope wash over her.

"Ms. Salisbury, please call your next witness." Tinisha called Brenda to the stand, and the bailiff swore her in.

Looking directly at Brenda, Tinisha said, "Can you tell us what took place on January 27, of last year, on Friday evening at 5 PM?"

"I got off work and drove directly to Firestone Tire to have my brakes serviced."

"And what happened when you arrived at the tire shop?"

"I requested to get my brake pads changed while I waited, but the request came back denied. I was told they could change the pads the next day."

"And what did you do then?"

"I immediately called my friend Virginia to tell her about my dilemma because we had planned for me to get my brake pads changed, drive to her home, and then make our way to Los Angeles."

"And what happened when you called Virginia?"

"She told me she could have her driver drive us to Los Angeles instead, and she suggested I just leave my car at the shop until I returned back home, so I could have the repairs done."

"So what did you do?"

"I called my husband to see what his suggestion was. He agreed with Virginia, and

I asked the desk clerk if someone could take me home."

"And did they give you a ride home?"

"Yes, they did."

"Then what happened?"

"At about 6 PM, I was picked up from my home by my friend Virginia Boswell's driver."

"And was Virginia also present with the driver?"

"Yes, she was."

"And what was your destination?"

"I was accompanying my friend to the city of Los Angeles to the City of Hope for her chemotherapy session."

"What time did you arrive at the city of hope?"

"Approximately midnight."

"What happened when you and Virginia arrived?"

"We were shown to our room by the night staff, and the next morning at eight o'clock, Virginia had her first treatment of the day."

"At any time did you leave the facility?"

"No, I did not."

"Is there anyone who can vouch for your whereabouts?"

"Yes. Maurice Pullman, the nurse who attended to Virginia, the receptionists, and the cafeteria worker who delivers the meals to the guest rooms."

"How long were you and Virginia at the City of Hope?"

"We stayed there until Sunday evening at 5 PM."

"Did you speak to your husband between the time you left home to the time you left the City of Hope?"

"Yes, I spoke with him three times. We always made a point to call each other when we were in transition from one location to another. So, once Gin… I mean Virginia and I arrived to the City of Hope, and I was settled into the room, I gave him a call. The next day, sometime in the afternoon, I believe it was around lunchtime, I gave him a call. He did not answer, but I did leave a message. He called back about twenty minutes later. Then, when we departed the city, I called him to let him know we were preparing to make our way back."

"Can you state your whereabouts on Sunday, January 29, between 10 PM and midnight?"

"At 10 PM, I was on the road returning to San Francisco from Los Angeles."

"And were you still on the road at midnight?"

"No, I made it back to San Francisco between 10:30 and 10:45 PM."

"Mrs. Jimenez, when you made it back to San Francisco from Los Angeles did you go home?"

"No, I went to Virginia Boswell's home."

"Did you make it a point to call your husband when you returned back to Ms. Boswell's home?"

"Yes, I did."

"And, did he answer?"

"No, he did not."

"And did that concern you?"

"No, I was not concerned at all. My husband went to sleep habitually at 10 PM."

"So, you assumed he was asleep?"

"I did."

"Can you give us a step-by-step account of your whereabouts from the time you arrived to the Boswell home to the time you actually made it to your home?"

Brenda proceeded to give a detailed account of how she assisted Virginia with being comfortable that night once they had arrived back to Virginia's home and had settled in. Afterward, she took a long bath and soaked in the tub. After her bath, she made a light snack, ate it, and then went to bed herself.

In the middle of the night at approximately two o'clock, she went into Virginia's room to check on her to make sure she was comfortable in her bed and warm enough. Next, she administered Virginia's medication.

The next time she woke up, it was four o'clock. After getting dressed, she went downstairs to make herself a cup of coffee.

At 4:20, she went into Virginia's room to find her sitting up and taking her meds. Brenda packed her bag and called a cab to pick her up to take her home. While she waited for the cab, she called her husband to let him know she would be on her way soon because they had planned for him to drop her off at work before he made his way to work. However, he did not answer his phone.

At that point in her account of the events of the morning she returned home, she paused, and the entire courtroom was still and not a sound was made. Tinisha waited a few seconds for Brenda to continue, but Brenda did not resume her testimony.

Prompting Brenda to continue, Tinisha asked, "Did the cab finally arrive to take you home?"

"Yes, it did."

"And, what time did you arrive home?"

"Right around five that morning."

"And Mrs. Jimenez, what did you find when you arrived to your home?"

"I entered my home through the front door and called out to my husband, but he did not answer me." Brenda paused trying to collect herself, as the tears fell rapidly from her eyes. Tinisha immediately grabbed the box of Kleenex from the defense table that she had brought with her in the event Brenda became emotional while giving her testimony.

"Mrs. Jimenez, do you need a brief recess?" Judge Hanson inquired.

"No, Your Honor," Brenda responded respectfully, as she lifted her head. "I appreciate it, but I really would like to continue."

"Very well. You may continue," Judge Hanson responded sympathetically.

Brenda nodded quickly as she scanned the audience. Her eyes locked with Javier's eyes. She felt a sense of calm just by his very presence. Then, she looked up, and her eyes met Tinisha's eyes. She felt confident that she could go on with her testimony at that moment.

"What did you do when you did not get a response?"

"I sat my overnight bag near the front door, placed my handbag on the table, and went upstairs to the bedroom. I was thinking my husband was asleep in our bed. I thought he had overslept," Brenda stammered.

"What happened when you arrived to the bedroom?"

"Well, nothing. He wasn't there," she said, dabbing at her eyes.

"And was the bed made or unmade?"

"It was made."

"Could you tell if the bed had been slept in?"

"Yes, the bed had been slept in at some point since I left on Friday."

"How do you know the bed was slept in if the bed was made when you saw it on Monday morning?"

"I know the bed was slept in because I know how I make the bed and how my husband makes the bed. And when I left on Friday evening, the bed was the way I made it that morning. But when I saw the bed on Monday morning, it was the way he makes it."

"So, what did you do then?"

"I went back downstairs and went to the garage to see if his car was there."

"And was it?"

"Yes, his car was parked in its usual spot."

"Then, what did you do?"

"I walked from the garage to the den. And, that's when I saw him."

"What was he doing?"

"He was lying on the couch with an afghan pulled over him."

"Did you find that strange?"

"Yes, I did. It wasn't strange for him to fall asleep on the couch with the afghan. However, it was strange for him to sleep there the entire night."

"So, what did you do then?"

"I walked over to him and shook him, calling his name. But, he did not answer, and when I lifted the afghan, that's when I saw the blood. And his skin was cold and clammy." That's when the tears started flooding out again, as Brenda's voice quaked.

"What did you do then?"

"I ran around to the other side of the couch and grabbed him and just held onto him for a few minutes. Finally, I let go, ran to get my phone from my handbag, and called 911. They asked me what the emergency was, and I told them my husband was dead and that they needed to send the police. I gave them my address, and I dropped the phone."

"Then, what happened?"

"Finally, the police arrived and the paramedics, and they were banging on the door and ringing the doorbell, and I finally opened the door. I guess I did not hear them at first. I might've been in a state of shock."

"Objection, Your Honor," the district attorney asserted.

"The witness has a right to testify about her own mental condition," Tinisha responded.

"Overruled," Judge Hanson responded, agreeing with Tinisha.

"What did the police find once they arrived?" Tinisha asked Brenda.

"They found a gunshot wound to my husband's left temple, and they said he was shot with a .45 caliber pistol."

"Did they question you?"

"Yes, they did."

"Did they arrest you at that time?"

"No, they did not."

"When did the police finally make the arrest?"

"They arrested me about a month later."

"On what grounds?"

"They said my alibi for the time of his death was unverified. And there is no one to confirm or deny my alibi."

"Couldn't your friend Virginia verify your whereabouts?"

"No…"

"Why not?" Tinisha prodded, trying to encourage Brenda to explain.

"Well, she had passed by the time I was arrested."

"I see," was all Tinisha could and needed to say. She had made her point.

"Your Honor, I have no more questions for Mrs. Jimenez at this time."

"The district attorney will have an opportunity for cross examination of the witness after lunch. Court will stand in recess until 1 PM."

After lunch, when court resumed, Brenda returned to the witness stand, and Melvin Hutchinson stood gazing at her with a non-descript look on his face.

"Mrs. Jimenez, in an earlier testimony from Monique Boswell, she stated she was out with friends from 11 PM on Sunday night until 4 AM on Monday morning. Do you agree with her stated timeframe?"

"Yes, I recall her leaving the house shortly after her mother and I had arrived back from Los Angeles. And, I heard her return when I was getting dressed."

"And did you speak with her?"

"No, I did not."

"And what was Virginia Boswell doing during that time frame?"

"She was in her room resting."

"So, there is no one who can say they saw you during the hours of 11 PM and 4 AM. Isn't that correct?"

"Well, Mr. Hutchinson, I would say you are correct. Virginia saw me when I administered her medication, but she is no longer with us. So, unfortunately, she cannot testify. But, what I find interesting is there is no one who saw me anywhere else either. Is there?"

The audience became completely quiet after Brenda's response. Caught off guard, Hutchinson responded, "Mrs. Jimenez, I will ask the questions."

Judge Hanson interrupted their exchange, "Well, do you have any other questions for the defendant?"

"No, Your Honor," Hutchinson said as he returned to his seat.

"Ms. Salisbury, please call your next witness."

"Your Honor, the defense rests."

"Mr. Hutchinson, are you ready to render your closing statement?"

"Yes, Your Honor."

"You may address the court."

12

Quickly glancing at his notes, Gonzalez began to speak. "Well, I have an update on the two Firestone employees who did not have their alibis corroborated."

"Sounds good. Let's hear it," Rafael said.

"Rocky Holmes is the one who had the landline, and I did receive his phone records this morning. During the time the fire was set, he was on a long-distance call to a number that belongs to his mother in northern Idaho."

"What was the duration of the call?" Rafael inquired.

"One hour and twenty minutes."

"Wow, that is a heck of a phone bill," Milford chimed in.

"And there is no one else who lives in his home that could've made that call?" Rafael probed further.

"According to Rocky, he has been a widower for two and a half years, and he has no children."

"Okay, and what was the name of the other employee?" Rafael asked.

"Alan Holmes," Gonzalez answered.

"Okay, and were you able to verify his alibi?"

"Well, he has a receipt from his cable company where he went onto the cable menu and ordered a porn movie. The receipt shows the date, time, and duration of the movie. It also shows if the whole movie was watched or if it was turned off prematurely."

At his last word, the three men could not help but to laugh at the possible implication of the word.

"Okay, but if you think about it," Rafael began, "if a person had premeditated the fire, wouldn't he try to give himself an alibi?"

"Yes, I would say so," Gonzalez replied, "but wouldn't he choose an alibi that was more plausible? Like one that included his presence in front of other people?"

"I see where you're going with this," Milford interjected. "So, let me jump in and share what I found out about one of the other employees."

"Go right ahead," Rafael responded.

"Well, one of Joshua Middleton's closest friends was Bernie Matheson, and he has an alibi- being at his son's baseball game, along with some of the other parents. However, when I was talking to Mike Rye, I recall him mentioning that Bernie showed up late to the game, in the second inning to be exact."

"Did Bernie mention it himself during his interview?" Rafael inquired inquisitively.

"Well, I conducted his interview," Gonzalez said, "and, I do not recall anything about his timeframe of arrival to the game. He just made a point to say he was at the game, and I asked him what time it started and what time it ended. Then, he gave me those times."

"So let me see if I understand," Rafael said. "You're telling me that one of the other employees said Bernie was there but he arrived late, but when Bernie had his own interview, he didn't mention being late at all?"

"That's what I'm saying," Milford said, nodding his head.

"Very well then," Rafael began. "I say we take another look at Bernie and go by and have a conversation with him."

"Do we still have the mole in the Caruso organization?" Gonzalez asked, thinking of another angle.

"No, after the rumors of murders had calmed down, there did not seem to be a need for one, so we pulled him about six months ago," Rafael answered.

****

District Attorney Melvin Hutchinson slowly rose to his feet. His movements were demonstrative of someone who was performing before a large audience. He knew all eyes were on him, and he was ready to make an impression.

He stood perfectly erect before the jurors, looking each and every one of them in their eyes, scanning the look on their faces before he uttered a single word. "Ladies and gentlemen of the jury, you have heard many details over the past couple of weeks from each of the witnesses on both the side of the prosecution and the side of the defense. Allow me a moment to provide for you a short synopsis, a recap of sorts, to jog your memory regarding the facts presented by the district attorney's office. The deceased, Mr. Charlito Jimenez, was fatally wounded by a single gunshot to his temple, as he lay on a couch in his home on January 30 of last year. When the authorities arrived to his home, after having received a call from his wife, the defendant, Brenda Jimenez, they found no forced entry, no unlocked doors, and no unlocked windows. The only person who was in the home was one who has direct access to the home – the deceased's wife, the dependent, Brenda Jimenez."

Hutchinson pointed a finger in Brenda's direction, as if the jurors did not know who she was. At the mention of Brenda's name twice in a row and Hutchinson's gesture, all jurors looked in her direction, as well as everyone who was seated in the audience.

The looks and the stares made Brenda extremely nervous, as she felt tears begin to well up in her eyes. But, she was determined to keep her composure because she wanted to hear just how the district attorney would attempt to further spin the evidence in the state's favor. When Tinisha felt Brenda tense up, she placed her hand on Brenda's forearm to calm her.

Melvin Hutchinson continued his closing argument. "Also there was an eyewitness, who just a few hours before the call was made, saw Brenda's car leaving the scene of the crime. Again I remind you, no one had access to the Jimenez's home, except the deceased and his wife- the defendant. No one had access to her vehicle, except the deceased and his wife- the defendant. Furthermore, the defendant has no one to corroborate her alibi during the time of her husband's death, which according to the coroner's report was approximately between 3-5 AM. Yes, we heard from the taxi driver that dropped her off at her home in the 5 AM hour; however, there is no one to verify where Mrs. Jimenez was between 11 PM Sunday evening to 4 AM Monday morning. She could have very well left her friend's home at any time and returned prior to calling the taxi to take her to her home. Members of the jury, as you review the facts of the case, keep in mind that this beloved member of the community, who had no enemies and was loved by all who knew him, was murdered in cold blood. We must bring his killer to justice. I am asking you, based on the evidence presented here, to find the defendant Brenda Jimenez guilty of the cold-blooded murder of her husband Charlito Jimenez."

Just as Melvin had looked at the jury intently before beginning his closing argument, he stood silently for thirty seconds with an understanding and pleading look on his face, as he surveyed the jurors one last time before taking his seat.

"Ms. Salisbury, your closing argument please," asked Judge Hanson. Tinisha quickly rose to her feet and picked up her legal pad, but just as fast as she picked it up, she placed it back on the table, laying it face down. As she began to approach the jury box, she spoke loudly and confidently.

"Members of the jury, the district attorney has pointed out *some* facts while the other statements are simply *conjecture* and cannot be proven beyond a shadow of doubt. The defendant Brenda Jimenez is a grieving widow, who lost her husband in one of the most horrific ways anyone can lose a loved one. After caring for her ailing friend, month after month for over a year, going consistently with her to her cancer treatments, tired in her body and mentally exhausted, Brenda arrived home in the wee hours on the morning of January 30, to find what no one should ever have to find in their home: her husband shot to death, lying on a couch where they had spent so much quality time together. In a state of shock, she called the authorities, summoning them to their home. One month later, to Mrs. Jimenez's dismay, the authorities once again showed up on her doorstep, but that time, they were there to arrest her for the murder of her husband because her alibi could not be verified. Two days before they made their arrest, Virginia Boswell, Mrs. Jimenez's dear friend succumbed to her about with cancer. As a result, she was not able to provide evidence that her friend was indeed in her home during the hours that someone- not my client- went into the Jimenez home and shot Charlito Jimenez. But the district attorney has an eyewitness who claims he saw my client's car leave her home at approximately 3:30 that morning. However, my client's car was in the shop, and according to the shop owner's daughter, there is no possible way that my client could have gone to the shop, retrieved her vehicle, driven to her home, and returned the car back to the shop because her car was secure behind the gates that surrounded the property. Ladies and gentlemen, the district attorney has produced no motive and no murder weapon. Therefore, there is insufficient evidence for my client's arrest and also for a conviction of first-degree murder or even manslaughter. Because there has not been a preponderance of the evidence shown on the part of the district attorney's office, no motive, and no alibi, you must find my client, Brenda Jimenez, innocent of all charges."

After Tinisha had finished her closing argument, Judge Hanson released the jurors from their seats and instructed them to go back to the jury room. They would be transported back to the hotel in which they were being sequestered for the duration of the trial. They would meet in the jury room first thing in the morning to begin deliberations. Once the jury had been excused, Judge Hanson explained to both parties that they would be contacted as soon as the jury had reached a decision.

As expected, the media was waiting outside the courtroom, ready to pounce on Brenda, but Tinisha was armed and ready to ward off their questions. As Tinisha and Brenda pushed their way through the crowd, ignoring the news reporters' questions, Brenda's eyes scanned through the crowd, looking for Javier's face.

With tears blurring her vision, she thought she had simply missed him and maybe had passed him somewhere along the way. However, by the time she and Tinisha had made it to the underground parking structure, and Tinisha had safely walked Brenda to her car, Brenda assumed Javier would appear before she pulled away. Again, she was disappointed to not see Javier anywhere in sight.

Disappointedly, she started her car and pulled out of the parking space. When she reached the edge of the structure and prepared to drive out into the street, more reporters surrounded her car, banging on the front hood and tapping on the window, attempting to get an interview or at least one question answered.

"How do you feel now?" one reporter asked.

"What do you think the verdict will be?" another reporter yelled.

The only thing Brenda wanted to do at that moment was to be safe behind the walls of her home. Finally, she had reached the point in the trial where all of the evidence had been presented and all the witnesses had provided their testimonies. She honestly did not know how to feel. She was relieved she would not hear anymore testimonies and that her testimony had been given. But, she could not get a sense of what the verdict would be.

When she pulled onto her driveway, pressing the button of the garage door opener and entering the garage, she glanced across the street to Javier's home. To her surprise, his truck was parked in his driveway. Quickly, a thought ran through her mind to go over there and knock on his door. But she would never darken the doorstep of a woman when she had been sleeping with the woman's husband. That would be of the utmost disrespect, and Brenda would not do it.

But, she couldn't understand why he would leave on the last day of the trial when he had been there all the other days without fail. Not being able to come up with an answer on her own, Brenda decided not to speculate and to simply give him a call and let him explain his absence. Once she was settled inside, she took out her cell phone and dialed Javier's number, as she stood in her family room looking through the blinds at his house.

He did not answer his phone, and as she prepared to leave a message, she noticed his daughter's car was parked in the driveway next to his truck, and on the street in front of the house, his son's car was parked. Brenda decided against leaving a message because something inside her told her something was seriously wrong, and it must be concerning Javier's wife Maria. Something had caused him to leave the courthouse and the children to come to their parents' home. Without even thinking about it, Brenda began to pray for Maria.

****

When Tinisha left the courtroom, after leaving the parking structure, she immediately placed a call to her husband, letting him know she had successfully presented her closing statement and the decision was now resting in the hands of the jurors. She told

Rafael she was headed to the hospital to see her father and to find out when he would be released. The doctor had said he should be able to be discharged by the end of the week. Tinisha, her mother, and her father were all hopeful that his recovery would allow for his release. Rafael told Tinisha he would meet her there approximately an hour later; then, they could go out to dinner if she felt up to it. She agreed and disconnected the call.

****

At the hospital, Pastor Oglebee was feeling a little grumpy. He was tired of being confined to his bed and to a single room. He wanted to move around, see something different other than the dandelions someone decided were great for wall décor. His wife had tried to cheer him up, or at least change his mood, by bringing some of his favorite books to the hospital.

But, Richard refused to look at them long enough to become enveloped in them. It was more than just being at the hospital. The truth was, he was concerned about being away from the church. Normally, when he wasn't able to be at Sunday worship service or at the weekly Bible study, he would have Tinisha fill in. However, that time around, he knew the murder trial had her full attention, and he would not be responsible for adding more stress to her already stressful days, especially when she was with child.

Jolted from his thoughts, a voice brought Richard back to his sterile environment. It was his daughter, the apple of his eye. As Delores eyed her husband, she watched his demeanor change, as a smile covered his face. And, as an involuntary reaction, a smile covered hers also.

13

Not long after meeting with Captain Salisbury and receiving his instructions, Detectives Milford and Gonzalez headed to the Matheson home to meet with Bernie without notification. When Bernie answered the door and saw two police detectives standing there, who introduced themselves as Detective Milford and Detective Gonzalez, he was surprised, to say the least. A little nervous, he invited them into his home, asking what their visit was about. He could not bear it if they had more bad news. He was still dealing with the death of his friend and the loss of his job.

Once the detectives were inside, Bernie invited them to have a seat. Looking around, Milford opted for a seat on the rather worn couch, and Gonzalez sat in an equally worn

Lazy Boy recliner that was permanently slightly reclined. To prevent from sitting awkwardly, Gonzalez sat on the edge of the seat. Milford took the lead. "Mr. Matheson, we need to review the details of the night of the Firestone fire. I understand you were at your son's baseball game that evening. Is that correct?"

"Yes, that is correct," Bernie said, with a questioning look on his face.

"What time did the game start, Mr. Matheson?"

"The game started at six o'clock."

"And what time did you arrive, Mr. Matheson?"

"I was there at about six o'clock," Bernie answered, looking directly at the two detectives.

"Mr. Matheson, according to some of the other parents who were also at the game, you arrived late," Gonzalez interjected.

"So, are you sure you were there when the game started?"

Bernie said with his head down, as though he was deep in thought, "Actually, no. I may have been a little late."

"What time did you leave work that day, Mr. Matheson?"

"I got off at 5:30 when the shop closed."

"And, did you go directly to the park?"

"No. I stopped at the supermarket to pick up some Gatorade for the team. Oh, yes I remember. I had left my wallet at home, so I came home to grab it and went back to the store. So, yes. I was a little late to the game."

"What time would you say it was when you actually made it to the park after going home to get your wallet and going back to the store to get the Gatorade?" Milford inquired.

"I would say 6:30-6:45."

After listening to Bernie's contradictory answer, Milford and Gonzalez exchanged glances before standing, thanking Bernie for his time, and excusing themselves. Once they were back in their car, Milford spoke up first.

"I'm getting a weird vibe from that guy."

"Well, it just sounds like he had his time mixed up," Gonzalez said.

From his living room window, Bernie watched the detectives as they descended the driveway, entered their vehicle, and left his property. He couldn't help but wonder what was going through their minds.

On the way back to the precinct, Milford and Gonzalez decided it would be best to run a background check on Matheson. Milford sensed something was going on with Bernie, while Gonzalez wasn't quite sure, but he certainly respected his partner's opinion. Milford put a call in to Captain Salisbury to request the background report, and subsequently, Rafael made the official request to have the information available for the detectives upon their return.

When the detectives walked into the precinct, the desk clerk handed Milford a folder with the word 'Confidential' labeled on the outside. He automatically knew what it was. He glanced over his shoulder to

Gonzalez and headed to his desk with Gonzalez following directly behind him.

Anxious to get to the report, Milford took a seat at his desk, flipped the folder open, and quickly scanned the contents, flipping page after page after page.

"Wow," he said. "Mr. Matheson has been in trouble with the law since he was fourteen years old." Gonzalez raised his eyebrows but did not say a word. He waited for Milford to continue. "It looks like he was involved in petty theft and sent to juvenile hall, but later as an adult, he was arrested for home invasion and burglary and then grand theft auto, both of which he was convicted of and spent eight years in the state penitentiary."

"So, when did he get out?" Gonzalez asked.

"About two years ago. Hey, didn't someone say Bernie and Joshua had been friends for about twenty years?"

"Yes, I believe so. I think both Bernie and Joshua's wife Susan mentioned something about their longtime friendship."

"You know there is something fishy about this whole thing. Look, if ten years ago Bernie began serving a sentence that lasted for eight years, and then, he came out and began working at Josh's place but they've known each other for twenty years, Josh knew him before he went in. I say we check Joshua's record also and see what he was up to before he became the owner of Firestone."

"Yeah, and what would that prove, seeing that he is the victim here?"

"Yes, but if Bernie had anything to do with the fire, maybe it was deep rooted back to something that went on before Bernie went to jail. Maybe, this was premeditated and in the works for some time."

As Milford continued to survey Bernie's file, Gonzalez went to Rafael's office to request a background report on Joshua Middleton and explained his reason for doing so. Within minutes, the report was produced, and the desk clerk delivered the file to Gonzalez in Milford's office. Gonzalez promptly opened the file and began to peruse the contents. He learned Joshua, like Bernie, had been in juvenile hall for petty theft. There were no other convictions listed after that, but he had to wonder if somehow Bernie and Joshua had both been involved in the home invasion robberies for which Bernie had been convicted.

To get more information on the home invasion robberies, Milford and Gonzalez dug deeper into the files and learned Bernie indeed had an accomplice, but the accomplice had remained unnamed. At that point, the two detectives began to speculate that both Joshua and Bernie were involved in the robberies because Joshua also lived in the neighboring community where the robberies were committed, but only Bernie was convicted. That led them to believe that Bernie had set out for revenge upon Joshua because he had to serve eight years in prison while Joshua was free to open a business and be with his family.

They realized it was only speculation, but they were desperate to find a reason the fire had been set at Joshua's business and his life had been lost. So far, all other employees and all other avenues for possible suspects, such as Tommy Caruso, had been quelled. At that point, Bernie was the only lead they had to go on, and they wanted to make sure the lead did not run cold.

14

On Thursday, February 3, as James was walking out of the building, after delivering a package, his cell phone rang. Looking down at the caller ID, he did not recognize the number but decided to answer the call anyway, just in case it was Bernadette calling from the center. He knew she could only have one call out a day, and he certainly did not want to miss her call. But after answering the phone, he was surprised when he did not hear Bernadette's voice on the other end.

The pleasant voice said, "May I speak with James Devine?"

"This is James speaking."

"Oh, Mr. Devine. I'm glad I caught you."

"This is Sheila calling from Willow Brook Springs apartments. I just wanted to let you know that your application has been approved, and we will have a new vacancy on February 15, if you would like to take the one-bedroom apartment you looked at." Sheila paused to give James a chance to reply.

"Sheila, I am very much interested in the apartment, but please tell me what the requirement is to move in? I'm sorry I don't remember. I looked at so many apartments, and each one had different requirements."

"Oh, it's no problem, Mr. Devine. All you will need is first month's rent of $1050 and the $400 deposit."

James did a quick calculation in his mind, and new he already had the deposit covered, and he would get paid at the end of the following week, so it should not be problem. Lenny had permitted James to work extra hours because the courier service was still shorthanded. He knew James was trying to move and make a better life for himself and his girlfriend, so he was happy to oblige, plus it lifted a great load off his shoulders - literally.

Speaking quickly, James accepted Sheila's offer, and they went through the rest of the details. Once James completed the call, he contemplated whether or not he should visit Bernadette and share the good news with her. He wanted to give her all the motivation she needed to be successful in her treatment program. After mulling it over, he thought it would be a good idea, and he would go see her the next day, as they were only allowed visitors on Friday night, which was family night.

****

After not hearing from Javier on Tuesday after court and all day Wednesday, Brenda was suddenly jolted awake from a light nap when her cell phone rang. Answering the call, she heard Javier's deep voice, which sounded broken and sad.

"Brenda, how have you been?"

"Ummmm, I've been okay. I guess. Just waiting to hear the outcome of the trial."

"I know. I am so sorry I had to leave suddenly on Tuesday, but..." Javier's voice trailed off, and Brenda waited patiently to see what his next words would be.

"What happened, Javier? Is everything okay?

"No, Maria is gone," was all Javier could manage to say.

Brenda could hear his soft sobs over the phone, and she knew his heart was broken.

"Are you okay, Javier? What do you need me to do? Have you made all the final arrangements?"

"Yes, Maria had gone over all the details with me and our children when she was first diagnosed. So, everything is in motion now. Bren, it's just so strange walking by the room and not seeing her in there. I knew this day was coming, but to actually experience it is really strange. Maybe, I shouldn't be talking to you about it."

"No, you can talk to me about anything. I know how you feel with the loss of someone you have been with for so long," Brenda said, thinking about Charlie's absence.

"Yes, I knew you would understand," Javier said. They both fell silent not knowing what to say next.

Breaking the silence, Brenda said, "Do you want to come over? When was the last time you ate?"

"Uhh, I don't really feel much like eating, but I know I probably should. There's plenty of food here that people from our church have been dropping off. It won't all fit in the refrigerator either."

"I completely understand," Brenda said compassionately.

Changing the subject, Javier asked, "What happened in court on Tuesday?" And without waiting for her to respond, he said, "I saw on the news that closing arguments were given."

"Yes, that's true. The jury is deliberating right now, and the court will call my lawyer once a decision has been reached."

"How do you feel about everything?" Javier asked.

"I'm not sure. I just really feel numb."

"I can imagine," Javier said. "But, we will continue to pray for the best."

"Absolutely," Brenda agreed.

15

After Gonzalez and Milford had shared the new information they had on Bernie Matheson with Captain Salisbury, he performed and in-depth review of all the facts from the case. He didn't want to be hasty in making an arrest or moving in the wrong direction from being overly anxious to solve a case. Once he was satisfied there was probable cause, on Friday morning, Rafael instructed Gonzalez and Milford to take two officers with them to the Matheson home and arrest Bernie on the charges of arson and first-degree murder.

Within thirty minutes, the two detectives were pulling up in front of the Matheson home with a squad car directly behind them. Bernie was sitting on the porch in an old rocker, tossing back a beer even though it was only six o'clock in the morning. The porch light was still on from the night before and shone down on his slightly balding head.

As soon as he spotted the two cars, he stood to his feet, and his head and heart dropped. He wanted to walk inside the house, but his children were home. So, he decided to just wait it out, so they would not witness what was about to happen. It was one thing for the detectives to show up, but it was quite another for officers to show up as well. Bernie know all too well that could only mean one thing- he was about to be arrested. He had experienced that before. He never imagined he would go through it ever again.

One of the two officers drew his service revolver when he exited the vehicle and moved closer to the porch. He wanted to let Bernie know trying to escape would be a bad choice. Following directly behind him was the second officer, Milford, and Gonzalez.

"Bernie Matheson, you are under arrest. The charges are arson of the Firestone Tire Shop and first-degree murder of Joshua

Middleton," Gonzalez said, once he had reached the first step of the porch.

"Mr. Matheson, can you please turn around and put your hands behind your back," Milford requested, as the second officer took the bottle of beer from Bernie's hand. After Bernie turned around, the officer immediately placed the handcuffs on Bernie's wrists.

All of a sudden, the screen door opened, and Bernie's wife Josephine stepped out onto the porch. "What's going on here?" she asked in a loud voice, obviously bewildered to see an officer with his gun trained on her husband, as he was having handcuffs administered to his person.

"Babe, it's okay," Bernie said in a barely audible voice.

"What is the charge?" Josephine asked the detectives, ignoring her husband's statement.

"Arson of Firestone Tire and first-degree murder," Gonzalez answered. Josephine placed both hands over her mouth, as she tried to stifle a scream, as tears leaped from her eyes. She looked toward the front door, checking to see if the children were getting wind of what was going on.

"I'll call a lawyer," she said to Bernie, in a shaky voice. Bernie only nodded his head, while still holding it down.

"Where will he be held?" she asked Gonzalez.

"San Francisco Police Department, Third Precinct on Mariposa Blvd," Gonzalez explained.

Josephine gave a slight nod, went into the house, and closed the front door, keeping the commotion that was occurring outside from being witnessed by the children inside. As Bernie watched his wife turn away and walk inside, he couldn't tell if she thought he was guilty. He continued to hold his head down, as he could not believe the scene that was playing out before his very eyes.

The officer guided Bernie down the steps, leading him to the squad car. The other officer opened the back door, and Bernie stepped inside. Meanwhile, Milford and Gonzalez entered their vehicle. When all five men were inside the two vehicles, they headed back to the precinct.

****

On the other side of town, Tinisha was getting dressed, preparing to go to the hospital and assist her mother with gathering all of her father's belongings because he was being discharged that morning. He had accumulated so many additional items that Delores was required to take an extra suitcase to transport them all back home. She had a mind to throw them all away, but her husband would not hear of it.

After being in the hospital for over a week, Pastor Oglebee was anxious to get home and back into his own personal space. The hospital staff had treated him kindly, but there was nothing like being in the sanctity of his own home.

Finally ready to head out, Tinisha picked up her handbag, cell phone, and car keys. Reaching for the doorknob, she suddenly turned around and placed everything back on the sofa table. She walked into her bathroom and assumed the position she found herself in once a week since she had first learned she was pregnant. She knew when Rafael had fixed her breakfast that the pork sausage patty would not be agreeable to the baby. It was certainly tasty to her tongue, and she had savored every bite of it, but for some reason, she always experienced nausea after eating it.

Once she was done expelling her food, she proceeded to leave her home and head toward the hospital.

****

When Captain Salisbury received notification that Bernie Matheson was in custody and had been seated in an interrogation room, he quickly made his way down the hall to meet Detective Gonzalez and Detective Milford to question Bernie.

When Rafael entered the room, he expected to have to work hard for a confession and was ready to take turns grilling Bernie until he 'cracked.' But to his surprise, Bernie was slumped over the table with tears running down his face. So many tears had fallen that a puddle had formed on the table.

Not really knowing what to make of the unexpected scene, Rafael looked at Milford and Gonzalez for a hint of what was going on. Milford walked Rafael back outside the room and said, "He keeps babbling, 'I didn't mean to,' over and over again."

"And what do you think that means?" Rafael asked.

"We were just about to find out."

"Let's do it," Rafael agreed, as they both returned to the interrogation room. Bernie was still blubbering, like an adolescent. Gonzalez had made him sit up, so they could try to make sense out of what he was saying.

"Explain what you mean when you say you didn't mean to do it," Gonzalez pressed.

"I didn't mean to kill him," Bernie said.

Without looking at the captain and the other detective, Gonzalez pressed forward. "You didn't mean to kill who?"

"I didn't mean to kill Josh."

"So, are you admitting to setting the fire and killing Joshua Middleton?" Gonzalez asked.

"Yes, but it was an accident. I didn't mean to kill Josh."

"And you didn't mean to send the fire either?"

"Well, yeah... I did set the fire. I was just trying to destroy the records."

"What records?"

"The clients' records."

"Why did you want to destroy the records?"

"Joshua and Susan were beginning to suspect that I had been taking the cars out after hours, and I did not want to lose my job, so I wanted to destroy the customer records that show the mileage for the cars."

"And why were you driving the customer cars after hours? It doesn't sound like it had anything to do with business," Gonzalez inquired.

"Just joyriding and running errands when my own car was out of commission," Bernie said with a disappointed look on his face.

"So, you're trying to tell us that you purposefully set the tire shop on fire because you want to destroy records because your boss and his daughter were getting wind of you taking the cars from the shop without permission? And that you did not mean to kill Joshua? How do we know you didn't mean to kill Joshua? Isn't it true that you were upset from having to serve eight years prison time and Joshua got off Scott free?"

"Why would I be mad at Joshua about that? He promised me if I went away, he would take care of my family when I was gone. So, when I got caught by the cops, I did not give them his name. I took the fall all by myself. And, he kept his word. If we were both gone away to prison, both our families would have suffered. So, I owe him my life. I did not mean to kill him." The tears began to flow faster once again, and the blubbering soon followed.

Milford took out a writing pad, placed it on the table in front of Bernie, and told him to write out his statement. From the looks of things, the statement would take a while to be written because Bernie's hands were shaking very badly. After about ten minutes with no luck of legible handwriting, Rafael suggested Bernie's statement be an audible recorded statement, so they could move things forward.

When the technician had finished capturing Bernie's statement on tape and was exiting the interrogation room, Bernie's lawyer showed up.

"I know you did not talk to my client without his counsel present, did you?" Anthony Green asked.

"Actually, we did. Mr. Matheson was properly Mirandized, and he waived his right to counsel, and freely, of his own volition, gave us his statement. You are more than welcome to listen to it."

Ignoring Captain Salisbury's remark, Mr. Green looked over at Bernie and asked, "Is this true, Mr. Matheson? Did you waive your right to counsel?"

"Yes, I did. I can't take the burden of bearing this alone anymore. I just want to be free from it. I did not mean to kill Joshua. He was my friend." And with those words, the sobs deepened, as Bernie's head fell on the table.

****

At S. F. Memorial Hospital, Delores and Tinisha had gathered Richard's belongings and were walking behind the nurse who was wheeling him down the corridor to the elevator. While they were waiting for the elevator, Tinisha felt the vibration of her cell phone through her handbag. She quickly removed it and saw that a call was coming in from the courthouse. Stepping away from her parents and the nurse, Tinisha pushed the button and answered, to find the courtroom clerk on the other line.

"Ms. Salisbury, the jury has returned with the verdict. Court will be in session at 1 PM this afternoon."

"Thank you, very much. I will notify my client."

After disconnecting the call, Tinisha immediately dialed Brenda's number and relayed the news to her. They planned to meet in one of the court's meeting rooms at 12:30 that afternoon before going into the courtroom to hear the verdict.

****

At the precinct, Rafael, Milford, and Gonzalez had a light celebration, rejoicing because they had closed another case. They couldn't believe after interviewing over twenty witnesses, talking to the victim's family, and going through file after file after file that the confession would come so easily.

"I guess that is what guilt can do to you," Rafael said, as the three men clinked their cans of Pepsi together.

****

In the court's meeting room, Brenda and Tinisha sat at a table discussing the possible verdicts. "Let's begin with the most positive verdict. If you are found *not guilty*, you will not be able to be tried again due to double jeopardy. Now, let's examine the worst case scenario. If you are found *guilty*, you will be sentenced to jail time, which for murder is twenty-five years to life, with the possibility of the death penalty because California is a death penalty state."

Tinisha paused to give Brenda time to reflect on the words she had just spoken. But not wanting too much time to lapse to allow

Brenda to become emotional, she continued on. "The third option is that the jury will not find you *guilty* or *not guilty* because of a deadlocked jury."

"So what happens in that case?" Brenda inquired, although Tinisha had covered all of the information before. But Tinisha knew Brenda's nerves were getting the best of her, so she did not mind answering her concerns.

"Well, if that happens, the prosecution could bring the charges up all over again, and you could face another trial, at which time you could be found *guilty* or *not guilty*."

"But what would cause us to go to a new trial?"

"If the district attorney comes up with new evidence, he could open up a new case or should I say continue the case. But, let us cross that bridge if we come to it. Let's go into the courtroom now."

Seemingly reluctant, Brenda rose from her seat, grabbed her handbag, and followed Tinisha into court.

Inside, everyone waited for the judge to enter and address the jury. Once Judge Hanson had made her entrance, she wasted no time with pleasantries. It had been a long week, and she knew everyone was anxious to begin the weekend.

"Madam Foreperson, in the case of the State of California versus Brenda Jimenez on the charge of first-degree murder of Mr. Charlito Jimenez, how do you find?"

Rising to her feet before speaking, the foreperson looked directly at the judge and said, "Your Honor, we were unable to reach a unanimous decision in this case."

"Madam Foreperson, if the jury were given more time, do you believe a unanimous decision can be reached in this case?"

"No, Your Honor. I do not. We are deadlocked."

"Thank you, Madam Foreperson. Ms. Salisbury, would you like to pole the jury?"

Tinisha rose to her feet. "Yes, Your Honor."

"All jurors who voted guilty, please elevate your hands," Judge Hanson ordered. Six of the twelve jurors lifted their hands. "Thank you for your service jurors. You are excused."

After the jurors left the courtroom, Judge Hanson asked the defendant Brenda Jimenez to rise. "Mrs. Jimenez, because of the hung jury, you are free to go, but keep in mind if the district attorney sees fit, he can bring the charges back to you again. Do you have any questions?"

"No, Your Honor. Thank you," Brenda responded, as the tears ran down her face. She did not bother to wipe them away. For the first time in over a year, she felt some semblance of peace.

16

On Friday evening, Tinisha and Rafael went out to dinner to celebrate both of their victories. Tinisha couldn't really say that a hung jury was a complete victory, especially if the district attorney built a new case against Brenda, but for the moment, she would see it as one. Rafael, on the other hand, knew that bringing Joshua Middleton's murderer to justice was a true victory. He was sure though when Bernie's wife and Joshua's wife and all of their children understood what happened on that fateful day, none of them would be pleased with Bernie's actions.

As they sat at the table at an Italian restaurant, Rafael allowed his wife to go first and tell him what happened in court earlier that afternoon. He listened intently as his wife told him about the verdict and how half of the jury thought Brenda was guilty and the other half did not. That made it hard to speculate what could possibly happen if the case went back to trial. For example, if only three thought Brenda was guilty and the other nine thought she was innocent, Tinisha wouldn't be as worried if they should go back to trial because the odds would be in her favor. But, with half-and-half seeing it on either side, guilty and innocent, it would be hard to gauge the jury the next time around. If there was a next time.

"So, even though Brenda was found "not guilty," the question remains as to who actually shot Charlie," Rafael said, becoming more and more perplexed by the case.

"That's true," Tinisha said. "And, that is why the district attorney will continue to dig. That is, unless the police come up with something," she said, looking in his direction. Rafael did not answer his wife's suggestion, but he was definitely tossing the idea around in his mind. He knew they had done a thorough job when they went to the house initially and when they began to question Brenda. Although the police department didn't think she was guilty, the district attorney's office must have. Why else would they bring a case against her?

"Well, we will just have to wait to see how this plays out," Tinisha said, as she began to enjoy her meal. "So, honey, tell me about your day. I hear you have some exciting news."

Rafael proceeded to tell his wife the information that Detectives Milford and Gonzalez brought to his attention about Bernie and how they subsequently went and made the arrest. Then, pausing for dramatic fact, he went into the details of how Bernie cried throughout his confession of how he set fire to Firestone Tire and accidentally killed his best friend Joshua in the process.

"What made him set the fire in the first place?" Tinisha asked, as she grabbed another breadstick, without breaking her gaze on her husband, as she was hanging on his every word.

"He said he wanted to cover his tracks because Joshua and Susan were getting suspicious about him driving the customers' cars after hours." With those words, Tinisha dropped her fork and almost choked on her breadstick. Her choking caught the attention of the patrons at the surrounding tables. Rafael jumped up quickly to pat his wife on the back. She lifted her hand to communicate to him that she was okay, as she swallowed the bread. Before speaking, she reached for the glass of water to clear her throat.

"Babe, what's wrong?" Rafael asked.

"You do remember me telling you that Brenda's car was being serviced at Firestone tire at the time her husband was killed, right?"

"Yes, I think so. So, what's going on?"

"One of the witnesses said he saw Brenda's car coming out of her driveway the night Charlie was murdered. But Brenda's car was at the shop. Now, you're telling me that this Bernie guy was taking the customers' cars in the evening or after hours and driving them around town? That seems like too much of a coincidence."

"So, are you trying to tell me you think Bernie has something to do with Charlie's death?"

"Well, so far no one has come up with any other explanation. The district attorney is trying to make it seem as though Brenda left Virginia's house, somehow got into the Firestone locked gated parking lot, took her car, drove to her house, and killed her husband. However, don't you think it would be more plausible for someone who already had access to the parking lot to get the car, drive to her house, and kill her husband?"

"It may be more plausible, but what would be Bernie's motive for killing Charlie Jiminez?"

"Well, honey, I'm going to leave that to you professionals to find out." And with those words, she picked up her fork and resumed consuming her meal.

When James walked into the treatment center, he was grinning from ear to ear. He was truly excited about his visit with Bernadette, and he could not wait to tell her the good news about the apartment they would be moving into upon her completion of the program.

When he walked up to the desk to check in before going into the meeting room for family night, the receptionist said, "Good evening, sir. Please sign in here and tell me who you are here to see." James picked up the pen and signed his name into the visitor's book and told the receptionist, "I am here to see Bernadette Matheson."

After checking her computer, to ensure there was a client by that name, the receptionist turned back to James and said, "Go right through those doors, sir," as she pointed to a set of double doors to the right of her. James nodded, said thank you, and made his way to the double doors. Once inside the room, James saw various tables spread around with games on each and a buffet set up with what appeared to be great-tasting food. At the sight of the food, his stomach began to growl, causing him to realize he had not eaten since lunch time. Then, he spotted Bernadette and made his way over to her.

When she realized someone was walking in her direction, she looked and stood to meet him. James noticed how much better she looked compared to when she had begun the program at the beginning of the week. Her color had returned to her skin, and her face looked fuller. When James reached Bernadette, he held out his arms for an embrace. Bernadette willingly accepted his hug and squeezed him tightly.

Bernadette invited him over to the buffet, so they could fix a plate before having a seat. Anxious to satisfy his hunger, James followed behind Bernadette. After making themselves a hearty plate, they returned to the table where Bernadette had been seated.

Making small talk and enjoying their meal, they were interrupted by a sudden hush that fell over the room when a news bulletin came on the several TVs there were mounted on the walls around the room. Newscaster Peter Fallon was sharing the latest news in the Jimenez murder trial and an update on the Firestone fire. Bernadette grew agitated and angry, after hearing the jury for Brenda's trial was hung and she was able to go free. But when she heard Bernie Matheson, her brother, was arrested for the fire and the death of his best friend Joshua Middleton, she lost her dinner all over the table.

She was so hard to console that the staff had to take her into a separate room to calm her down. James knew Bernadette and Bernie were close, but he had no idea what was causing her reaction to his arrest. They both knew if Bernie continued his shenanigans that he would end up back in jail sooner or later, so James did not understand why Bernadette was surprised. He was just thankful that neither one of them had been involved with any of those shenanigans lately.

When James was finally able to see Bernadette again, she held his hand and whispered, "He is going down for murder. He is going down for murder." James did not utter a word, but in his mind he was saying, *Well yeah, of course, because Joshua Middleton is dead.*

****

After dinner, Rafael dropped his wife off at home and made his way quickly to the precinct. Waiting for him were Milford and Gonzalez. Rafael shared with them what he and Tinisha had discussed regarding Bernie and driving customer cars. After their lengthy discussion, Milford left to go see Bernie in the holding tank to question him further.

Once Milford was face-to-face with Bernie and began to question him, Bernie knew it was one thing to admit to accidentally killing someone, but it would be another thing altogether to admit to premeditated murder. So, he said nothing.

****

Thankful that Bernadette's bout of hysteria had quieted, James prepared to leave. Bernadette stopped him, grasped his hand tightly, and said, "I can't let him go down for me. It is all my fault. He did it for me." James did not understand what was going on with Bernadette, but he knew one thing – he did not like what he was hearing.

Very cautiously, James leaned over Bernadette and said, "Honey, what are you talking about?" Bernadette, with tears in her eyes said, "He killed Charlie because of me." Behind James, a tray of medication went crashing to the floor. Startled, James jerked his head around to see who or what had caused the commotion. One of the nurses was standing behind him with her hands covering her mouth and a metal tray, with small cups of pills, was strewn across the floor. Due to the popularity of the Jimenez case, everyone knew Charlie by name even if they had not ever heard of him before. So, when the nurse heard Bernadette's statement, she knew whom she was referring to. Immediately, without picking up the medication, the nurse turned and fled from the room. James knew she was going to alert the authorities, and there was nothing he could do to protect Bernadette. The secret she had been keeping had been revealed.

When the tray of medication had landed on the floor, Bernadette had lifted her head from the pillow to see what the noise was. When the nurse ran from the room, Bernadette just dropped her head back onto the pillow. She made no attempt to get up and escape.

Not much later, the police arrived at the treatment center to respond to the call that was made regarding information about the death of Charlito Jimenez. After speaking at length with the police officer, Bernadette had finally told the entire story surrounding Charlie's death and the actions that must have led up to the Firestone fire.

****

A year and a half ago, Brenda had been transferred to Bernadette's place of employment, an accounting firm, from one of the company's other branches. Bernadette had been on the verge of earning a promotion to senior accounting manager. However, because Brenda, who was also on the verge of a promotion, prior to her transfer, had received the one promotion that was available at their local office, Bernadette did not receive the long-anticipated promotion.

Bernadette was so devastated when the news came about the promotion and the increase in pay that would have come along with it that she began to suffer severe depression. Then, not much later, she had turned to drugs to drown her sorrows, after trying alcohol and its effects didn't seem to do the trick for her.

Bernadette's brother Bernie did not understand how his sister's life could change so quickly, from being a college graduate, who had attained her dream position, to being someone who was on drugs. As far as he was concerned, she was the successful one and he was the family screw-up. When his sister shared her misfortune with him, he had a strong desire to do something that would make her feel better although he had no idea what that would be.

Then one day, when Brenda Jimenez showed up at Firestone Tire to drop off her car, Bernie recognized her name as the person who had stepped in and taken the position that would have been his sister's. Bernie had a temper, and it had hurt him deeply to see his sister fall from grace and subsequently lose her job. So, after Brenda had to leave her car at the shop for the weekend, Bernie quickly devised a plan to visit her late in the night and take her in life because essentially, she had taken her sister's livelihood, joy, accomplishment, and health.

So, early Monday morning on January 30, Bernie left his home, while his wife and children were asleep, drove to Firestone Tire to retrieve Brenda's car, drove to her house, used the garage door opener to let himself in, and walked around until he heard snoring coming from the den. He proceeded to make his way toward the sound. When he saw someone lying on the couch, he assumed it was Brenda and fired the gun, aiming at the temple, without verifying the identity of the person. After the fatal shot, he looked and saw he had shot a man – Charlie – instead of Brenda. Moving quickly, he left without a backward glance.

After the officer had collected Bernadette's statement, he went back to the precinct and relayed all the information to Captain Salisbury who in turn shared the information with Detectives Milford and Gonzalez. Once again, they questioned

Bernie and filled in some of the details for him, alerting him that they had spoken with his sister Bernadette.

At the mention of her name, all Bernie could do was confess.

About the Author

Dr. Cassundra White-Elliott resides in California with her family, where as an English/Education professor she works for various community colleges and universities.

When writing, she writes with the direction of the Holy Spirit, in an effort to share with God's people all that He has for them.

In addition to teaching and writing, Dr. White-Elliott also serves as an evangelistic teacher. She is also the founder of International Women's Commission, a ministry that serves the needs of the entire person, by attending to healing the mind, body, soul, and spirit.

Dr. White-Elliott holds a Ph.D. in Education, a Master's in English Composition, and a Bachelor's in Education.

Dr. White-Elliott is also the founder of CLF Publishing, LLC. For your publishing needs, go online to www.clfpublishing.org.

OTHER BOOKS BY THE AUTHOR
(All books can be purchased at
www.creativemindsbookstore.com)

From Despair, through Determination, to Victory!

A lot can happen during a span of 40 years. The life of Dr. Cassundra White-Elliott has been anything but uneventful. From a fun-loving childhood sprinkled with incidents of abuse to a tumultuous young adulthood to a stable, secure adult life, she has experienced a full life, with much more to come. Her story is inspiring and motivating.

If anyone lacks hope, reading Dr. White-Elliott's autobiography will propel him/her into an attitude of "Maybe I can." This attitude, if nurtured and developed, will grow into an attitude of "Yes, I can." Throughout her life, Cassundra has always held in her heart the belief that she could achieve anything that she had a made-up mind to embark upon. She was determined to achieve her heart's desires, doing what God has called her to do. She takes no credit for herself. All the glory goes to God, for He is her driving force. In Him, she lives, moves, and has her being.

Through the Storm

Through the Storm was duly inspired by the avaricious cloud of depression that decided to hover overhead of my daily existence in the latter part of 2007. Although I found it extremely difficult, I was once again compelled to not be defeated by just another snare that the enemy, the trickster, set for me. Once again, or more appropriately I should say *continuously*, he has exerted pernicious efforts to snatch the very life out of me by causing me to wallow in despair and to believe that I had been overcome by failure when in actuality and all reality, I was just experiencing a temporary setback. During those cloudy days, I had to remind myself daily that even though I was a target of the enemy, I am and will always be a child of the Most High god, Jehovah, who is my rock, my stability.

Unleashed Anger, Anger Unleashed

As I prepared to embark upon the adventure of writing this book, I had to prepare myself to also be transparent. I have found that being transparent is required in order for healing to transpire, healing for all those that peruse the pages of this book and myself. And I may as well tell you that today, at the onset of this project, I have not been totally delivered from my condition of being an anger-filled person. However, I am definitely a work in progress. I have made strides with the assistance of my Lord and Savior, Jesus Christ, who is the head of my life. Without his love, guidance, and teachings, I would not be the woman of God I am today. I shudder to think where I could be instead and will therefore not entertain the thought.

Chapter Two
How Communication Works
Purpose: This chapter will explain the six primary components of communication, identifying their purpose and how they work together.

The Source

In oral communication, the source of information is the speaker. In a church setting, the foundation of the message is God's word, but it is a speaker's interpretation of God's word that is delivered to the audience. As speakers vary, the information may vary but should have a similar essence because the foundational text is the same.

The Message

The message is the collective set of ideas that the speaker (the source) wants to deliver and/or illustrate to the audience.

Where is Your Joppa?

Introduction

Where is Your Joppa? was written for the express purpose of illustrating God's call for obedience in the lives of believers with respect to the individual call that He has on each of our lives. As you read throughout the various chapters, notice that the emphasis is placed on our persistent disobedience in answering God's call in a specific area of our lives. We have become a people who are similar to the Israelites when they found themselves in the middle of the wilderness, following their exodus from Egypt. Before God, they murmured and complained about their current life conditions and failed to be obedient to God's statutes delivered through His servant Moses. Their persistent disobedience caused them to lose the opportunity to see and enter the Promised Land. I ask you, "What has your disobedience cost you?" "Was your disobedience worth what it cost you?" "Do you think about the souls you could have ushered into the kingdom of God?" These are some of the questions that I pray will be answered through your reading of the book.

Mayhem in the Hamptons

Romero and Yolanda optimistically plan for the day that is going to change their lives from being single persons to a couple who is united in holy matrimony. They, along with their parents, close friends and family, fly over to the infamous Hamptons, where only the rich and famous vacation, to have their dream wedding at the five-star Hampton Suites located on a peninsula in the Hamptons. Little do they know that their perfect day will turn out to be less than perfect when their wedding planner Mariesha Coleman suddenly goes missing!

A time when the newlyweds' lives should be filled with joy and the creation of wonderful memories, they are stricken with grief as they desperately try to find clues to help solve Mariesha's disappearance.

Mayhem in the Hamptons is a tale that shares how the horrors of a woman's past can come back to haunt her in more than one way and the impact it can have on anyone who gets in the way.

Preacher's Daughter

Tinisha, the daughter of a preacher, is a twenty-six year old God-fearing young woman endeavoring to complete law school so that she can make her mark in the courtroom. Working in one of the late-night clubs in Hollywood to earn money to pay her own way through school, Tinisha soon learns that life doesn't always go as planned.

Preacher's Son

Romero Turner is a private investigator with a promising future. As he continues to build his career, he is excited about the cases he undertakes. However, his father Pastor Theodore Turner has other plans for his son's life. In the midst of trying to save his client's husband from Sylvester Domingo, a ruthless crime lord, Romero must try to salvage his relationship with his father. He must decide if ministry or life as a detective is in his future.

Lord, Teach Me to be a Blessing!

Lord, Teach Me to be a Blessing! will change a person's mentality from being centered around "me, myself, and I" to focusing on "others."

The world system teaches us that it is acceptable to place ourselves above others in an attempt to get ahead and even to survive. Herbert Spencer coined the phrase '*survival of the fittest*' after reading Charles Darwin's theory of evolution. This concept of surpassing and outdoing others is the world's philosophy.

However, the word of God does not subscribe to or promote this self-centered ideology, and therefore, neither should believers. We must hold fast to the truths outlined in Scripture: "*Love thy neighbor as you love thyself.*"

After the Dust Settles

Throughout the journey of life, we all experience ups and downs and joys and pains. Most of us successfully find solutions to the situations/problems we encounter, but we often avoid dealing with the attached emotions. If we continue to ignore the emotions of pain, hurt, disappointment, anger, etc., we set ourselves up for destruction. Our families, our cultures, and our society tell us to be strong, to keep our chin up, and to grin and bear it. However, these methods of avoidance can lead us to strokes due to the undue amount of pressure we place on ourselves and/or mental illness from being unable to cope with the emotional baggage we have accumulated.

A Diamond in the Rough

A Diamond in the Rough Architecture Firm was built and is owned and operated by lead architect Kyra Fraser. For the last five years, Kyra has been extremely successful in business, but her love life leaves much to be desired.

Kyra has set high standards for herself and does not wish to take a man in any condition and attempt to make him over. She is looking for someone who is drama free, well educated, very cultured, fun-loving, good looking, self-motivated, and the list goes on.

Will Kyra find the man of her dreams, or will her dream just continue to be a dream?

As you delve into this page-turning novel, Kyra's reality will unfold as you are drawn into her world of design, love and office drama- which includes her best friend's husband who is looking for love in all the wrong places.

Just as our brain requires oxygen obtained from the air we breathe to sustain our mortal bodies, our spirit requires revitalization and encouragement in order to be strengthened each and every day of our lives. The revitalization and encouragement needed for the spirit of man comes directly from the word of God and assists us in walking according to the way of our heavenly Father. 365 Days of Encouragement provides a scripture a day for each day of the year. Along with the daily scripture is a brief note of commentary also for the benefit of edifying the saints of God.

It is my prayer that the people of God would live a fulfilled life through Christ Jesus. Knowing His word and understanding we can walk in the fulfillment thereof is empowering.

A Mother's Heart

A Mother's Heart shares the unconditional love of mothers through a compilation of testimonies. Each testimony serves as a tribute to a special mother. The children of the represented mothers have lovingly written about their childhood, young adult life and/or older adult experiences they shared with their mother. As you read the writers' reflections, you will feel the expressions of love exude from the pages.

Our advice to mothers is, "Be encouraged; the journey of motherhood may seem daunting at times and you may shed some tears, but your children will never forget the love you have shown them and instilled in them to share with others."

Broken Chains

Broken Chains is an in-depth survey of five life-changing tragedies that can and will serve as chains to bind us if we are not watchful and mindful of their potential effects. In our lifetimes, we may all experience death of loved ones, sexual abuse, broken relationships, promiscuity, and sickness and disease. These everyday life occurrences can have detrimental effects on the remaining years of our lives and change our existence, unless we deal with them in a healthy manner.

Broken Chains not only brings to light the detrimental effects of five life-changing tragedies, but it also shares how anyone who experiences them can be healed and delivered from their effects.

I Have Fallen

Do you know anyone who has committed his/her life to Christ but has done something unseemly that you would never expect a Christian to do? How did you feel about that person or what the person did? Did you pass judgment? What if that person were you? How would you feel if you made a misstep and no one forgave you and instead began to treat you differently? How do you feel when you are judged for past mistakes or lifestyles that are no longer part of your life?

This book shares four true stories of Christians who have made missteps during their walk with God. The purpose is not to air their dirty laundry, but to demonstrate our humanness and our vulnerability. None of us are exempt from making errors and falling into sin. It can happen to any of us.

The Bottom Line

The Bottom Line is a detailed review of the Book of Job. Much can be said about Job's experiences with the loss of his children and wealth and the subsequent return of it all in mass proportions. However, the telling of Job's story in the Holy writ was not intended to focus on the return of his wealth. Instead, the focal point should be on the bottom line of the entire situation.

When you experience trials or tragedies in your life, do you tend to focus on the trial itself, the result, or the bottom line?

"What is the bottom line?" you may ask. The bottom line is the message God is sending regarding the situation.

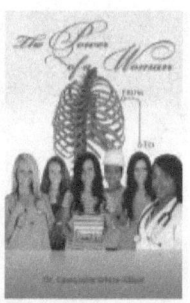

The ongoing conversation about the value of a woman is presented from a different perspective in *The Power of a Woman*. Dr. Cassundra White-Elliott presents a biblical perspective of women and compares it to the worldview of both yesterday and today. This comparison seeks to illustrate God's intended purpose for His uniquely designed creation: woman. Dr. Elliott shares God's truth about pre-imposed limitations set by man versus the limitations God Himself set for woman in addition to the wealth of liberality He gave her.

Women, let's take the blinders off, lift our heads up, and march forward, side by side with men, and bring glory and honor to God! Take your rightful place with a gentle smile and grace and be who God called you to be!

Set Free

If you possess habits and display characteristics that are unbecoming, debilitating, and hinder the desired progress in your life or that affect your relationships with others, Set Free will provide the steps you need to be healed and delivered, through the Word of God.

Deliverance is available to you! Claim your healing today and walk in victory!

Do You Know God?

Have you or someone you know ever felt alone, confused, or unsure about your walk with God or are you unsure of what being a Christian is all about? *Do You Know God?* is an excellent text for providing answers to many of your questions. This book introduces adolescents and young adults to God in addition to answer many of their questions about being a Christian. This book shares the testimonies of the trials and tribulations that other teens have experienced and how God prevailed in their lives. All the information that is shared on the pages of the book is based upon the Word of God and the scriptures are taken from the King James Version of the Bible. If you are interested in knowing more about God's Word or how to begin your Christian experience, this book is for you.

Daughter,
God Loves You!

"... for her price is far above rubies"
(Proverbs 31:10B)

Dr. Cassundra White-Elliott

Maybe you have heard the proclamation, "The world is going to hell in a hand basket!" Well, I believe I must concur.

However, I do not believe, we, the adult, mature believers—should sit idly by and allow our daughters (and our sons for that matter) to go with it! We must fight for our girls and young women, for they are the mothers of tomorrow, and some may even be young mothers today. Not only will they continue the human race, but also they can have bright futures in their careers and as leaders in our society. As they allow God to direct their paths and order their steps.

Daughter, God Loves You! is a earnest attempt to address many of the issues that plague our society and turn our daughters' heads away from God.

In this book, we dive head first into topics such as God's love, the importance and impact of education, the effects of social media, overcoming abuse, and the proper perspective of the future.

For the young adult women: Reading this book will empower you to have a bright prosperous future from being enlightened about the dangers that plague our society and how to avoid pitfalls, as you walk along the path God has paved for you.

I invite all of you to take this journey with me to save our daughters and yourselves (young women) from corruption, by being empowered with knowledge.

We must thwart the plan of the enemy. So, LET'S GO!

CLF Publishing, LLC.
www.clfpublishing.org

ISBN 978-0-9963971-9-9

Dr. C. White-Elliott's books are available at:
www.creativemindsbookstore.com
www.amazon.com
www.barnesandnoble.com

A Mother's Heart II shares the unconditional love of mothers through a compilation of testimonies. Each testimony serves as a tribute to a special mother. The children of the represented mothers have lovingly written about their childhood, young adult life and/or older adult experiences they shared with their mother. As you read the writers' reflections, you will feel the expressions of love exude from the pages.

The purpose of this book is two-fold. First, it honors those mothers who stood by their children through the trials of life and showered them with unconditional love. Second, the book is a source of encouragement for mothers who may feel inadequate and question whether or not they are actually suited for motherhood. Our advice to mothers is, *"Be encouraged; the journey of motherhood may seem daunting at times and you may shed some tears, but your children will never forget the love you have shown them and instilled in them to share with others."*

Mothers may not be perfect, but they are definitely unmatched by any other category of person on God's green earth!

The following authors are included in this compilation:
Edwin Baltierra, Shelia Bryant-Colbert, Jean Cedeno,
Ilse Guadalupe Hernandez, Haley Keil, Haley King, Johnathon Lopez,
Ronnette Moore, Allyson Marie Sanders, Lucas van den Elzen,
Daron C. White, Ashton Wilson, Jessica Yslas, and Vanessa Zavala.

CLF Publishing, LLC.
www.clfpublishing.org

Dr. Cassundra White-Elliott's books are available at:
www.creativemindsbookstore.com
www.amazon.com
www.barnesandnoble.com

ISBN 978-1-945102-02-8
90000

The journey from adolescence through puberty to young adulthood can be challenging and quite disconcerting for the average young lady. The changes that occur both mentally and physically can be both confusing and uncomfortable. However, the outcome of the changes can be beautiful! What she will experience during this time in her life is simply a *metamorphosis* - taking off the old and embracing the new. The process is similar to that of an awkward caterpillar that overtime develops into a beautiful, graceful butterfly.

The topics covered in this book (puberty, self-esteem, mental stability, goals, finances, and relationships) will assist young women (ages 15-23) in understanding the transformation they are enduring to prepare them for the life that lies ahead. After taking in the information, they will literally witness themselves evolve from princess to queen!

CLF Publishing, LLC.
www.clfpublishing.org

Dr. Cassandra White-Flora's books are available at
www.creativemindsbookstore.com
www.amazon.com
www.barnesandnoble.com

ISBN 978-1-945102-19-8

9 781945 102158

A Mother's Heart III shares the unconditional love of mothers through a compilation of testimonies. Each testimony serves as a tribute to a special mother. The children of the represented mothers have lovingly written about their childhood, young adult life and/or older adult experiences they shared with their mother. As you read the writers' reflections, you will feel the expressions of love exude from the pages.

The purpose of this book is two-fold. First, it honors those mothers who stood by their children through the trials of life and showered them with unconditional love. Second, the book is a source of encouragement for mothers who may feel inadequate and question whether or not they are actually suited for motherhood.

Our advice to mothers is, "Be encouraged; the journey of motherhood may seem daunting at times and you may shed some tears, but your children will never forget the love you have shown them and instilled in them to share with others." Mothers may not be perfect, but they are definitely unmatched by any other category of person on God's green earth!

The following authors are included in this compilation:
Yolanda Castro, Georgette Liel, Gate Thompson, Nicholas Harrison,
Juani Harrison, Ashleigh Morris, Jerry G. Martin, Jourdan Jewel,
Khalil Houston, Audrey Arblochi, Cathy Vines-Nichols, Akayla Clayton,
Dajénan Jackson, Quantanique Williams, Malik'em Redd, Abbeayah Nichols,
John Lary, Maria Guzman, Tyler Kowalski-Foley, Haley Koil,
Fernando Loucim, Elaine M. Tolentino, and Karen Butt.

CLF Publishing, LLC.
www.clfpublishing.org

ISBN 978-1-945102-16-5

Dr. Cassundra White-Elliott's books are available at
www.creativemindsbookstore.com
www.amazon.com
www.barnesandnoble.com